Blue Horse Mesa

Western Stories

Books by John D. Nesbitt

For the Norden Boys
Lonesome Range
Black Hat Butte
Red Wind Crossing
Rancho Alegre
Raven Springs
Coyote Trail
Black Diamond Rendezvous
Man from Wolf River
Not a Rustler
West of Rock River
North of Cheyenne
Poacher's Moon
Adventures of the Ramrod Rider
A Good Man to Have in Camp
Keep the Wind in Your Face
Shadows on the Plain
Field Work
Blue Horse Mesa: Western Stories
Antelope Sky: Stories of the Modern West
Seasons in the Fields: Stories of a Golden West

Two Novellas:
"Dead for the Last Time"
"Trouble in the Labor Camp"

Blue Horse Mesa

Western Stories

John D. Nesbitt

SPEAKING VOLUMES, LLC
NAPLES, FLORIDA
2016

Blue Horse Mesa Western Stories

ISBN 978-1-62815-471-9

for Pete, who was a good horse

Acknowledgments

"Rose of Durango" appeared as an Amazon Short in December 2007 and as a Western Trail Blazer e-book, April 2011.

"LeBlanc Station" appeared in *ReadWest: Stories of the American West* (ReadWest Foundation, 2012)

"Chugwater Charlie" appeared in *Cactus Country Anthology, Volume I* (High Hill Press, 2011).

"For the Love of Camille" appeared as a Kindle e-book in February 2012.

"Where the Water Once Ran" appeared in *Out West*, Summer 2007, and in *Coffee Cramp eZine*, December 2007.

"Emma's Purpose" appeared in *Out West*, 2006.

"Not Going Anywhere" appeared in *Cactus Country Anthology*, Volume II (High Hill Press, 2011).

"Night Falls at Lonetree" was first published as a Shirt Pocket book (Treble Heart Books, 2010).

"Song of Pierre" appeared as a Western Trail Blazer e-book, October 2011.

"Hap" appeared in *The Law of the Gun* (Pinnacle Books, 2010).

"Blue Horse Mesa" appeared in *Lost Trails* (Pinnacle Books, 2007).

Table of Contents

Rose of Durango

Rose of Durango began as an idea, or I might say she took form in my mind as a kind of picture. I first knew of her one day in late summer when my girl-friend Magdalena said her family was worried about a cousin who had gone north to work on a ranch. The woman had been gone for a couple of months, and no one had heard from her. Magdalena referred to the cousin as *Rosa de Durango*.

"Durango, Colorado?" I asked, keeping the conversation in Spanish as usual.

"Yes."

"Then I haven't met her."

"No. She is from the other side of the family."

"And Rosa Linda and your grandmother and the rest, how are they?"

"They are all fine, *gracias a Dios*."

Of the family I had met in Colorado Springs, I remembered Rosa Linda the best. My picture of her was of a smiling, cheerful girl who seemed always to have the shine of a recent bath. She favored yellow dresses, and she gave the impression of innocence—like a yellow rosebud, swelling but not yet opened. Her family made sure she never went anywhere alone.

The cousin from Durango, on the other hand, sounded like a working girl. If she went off by herself to take a job in a ranch kitchen, she was a different kind of rose.

"And where is the ranch where your cousin went to work?"

"In the place where you went, a little while back. Wyoming."

"Wyoming is a big place, and I got to know just a corner of it. Do you know the name of the ranch, or the town it is near?"

"The town is Hartville," she said, pronouncing it in Spanish so that it sounded like "Hardveel."

"I've heard of it."

"And the man is named Vermeelion or something like that."

"Vermillion. That's a name. It means bright red." As my eyes met hers, I said, "Nena, you seem to be well prepared with all the information."

Her eyes sparkled as she smiled. "You are so good at these things, *Yimi*. I thought you might have an idea."

True enough, I had been out to look for missing people a couple of times, and even though I didn't come back with good news, in each case I found what I was looking for, and more. "Does that mean you would like me to try to find her?"

"Not if you don't want to, and she may not be in any trouble at all."

"Wouldn't it be best if she was not in trouble?"

"Oh, yes."

"But it would still be good if someone could find out that much."

She smiled, as if to say I was getting the idea. "Well, yes."

I gave it a few seconds of thought. "I guess I can try. I need to know what she looks like. I don't suppose you have a picture."

"No, but I can describe her. Put her at my height, neither fat nor thin, *trigueña*."

"*¿Trigueña?*"

Magdalena passed her hand downward in front of her face. "Dark. Like my uncle Chanate. And long, black hair."

I recalled my friend Chanate, who took his name from the blackbird, and I imagined a woman with that complexion and a full head of dark hair. "Very well. How old?"

"Oh, I don't know. A few years older than I am."

"Twenty-five? Thirty?"

"Put it at thirty."

I nodded. The rose was beginning to take form—a red rose, fully opened and darkening, with the traces of time on the edge of the petals. "And her last name?"

"Aguilar—no, Méndez."

"Is she married?"

"No. Aguilar is from another part of the family. She is Méndez. I don't see her very much, and on this side we call her Rose of Durango."

Now the full image came up for me—a blend of the dark woman as Nena had described her and the dark rose as I had imagined it. From my past experiences I knew that when a fellow went to look for someone, he developed a sense of that person's manner of being, as they say in Spanish. At the same time, I knew that the image or picture did not always match

3

the person it turned out to be. But at least I had something to go on.

"I suppose I will leave tomorrow, then."

Magdalena's eyes had a soft glow as she said, "You are so good to help out, *Yimi*. We will miss you. May you have a good trip and a safe one. I'll wait for you."

Those last words were the best. "I hope to be back before the snow falls," I said.

She laid her hand on my forearm. *"Con el favor de Dios."*

That was Magdalena. She was no saint herself, but she never forgot about God.

* * * * *

The road to Hartville ran north out of Cheyenne through Horse Creek, Iron Mountain, and Chugwater. I traveled light and didn't waste time, keeping an eye on the mountains to the west and hoping the weather didn't make any big changes. The chokecherry bushes were turning red, and a few cottonwood leaves had gone to yellow, so I knew fall was on the way. I camped on Chugwater Creek the fourth night of my trip, and from that point on I felt I was getting into the real business of my journey.

Mid-way through the next day, I stopped at a roadhouse to give my little black horse a rest and to find out what I could. The proprietor served me up a meal of cold beef, hard biscuits, and warm beer, then stood back running his fingers through his beard as he plied me with questions.

"Where ya headed?"

"Up north."

"How far? Next ranch up?"

"A little farther."

"How far is that? Powder River country? Montana?"

"What's north of the Platte?"

"'Pends on which way you go. You got Orin, Douglas, Glenrock, then Casper if you hook around that way. Go the other way, you go to Hartville, or farther yet, you go on the other side of the Rawhide Buttes, on the way to the Black Hills. Go through Lusk."

"What's in Hartville?"

He wrinkled his nose. "Copper mine sort of peterin' out. Iron ore's doin' better. Red stuff there. What ya lookin' for?"

"Ranch work." I swallowed a dry lump of beef and tried to wash it down with the beer. "Also supposed to keep a lookout for the relative of a friend that came up this way."

"What kinda man? All kinds come through here."

"A woman, actually."

The man took his fingers out of his beard and said, "Ah."

"Mexican woman."

He sniffed. "She run off on someone, did she?"

"From what I understand, she came up here to work."

"Huh. Biggest hog ranch up this way is out by Fort Fetterman. They got Swedish girls, from what I hear, plus yer regular white girls, now 'n' then a Nigra. She might be there."

"I was given to understand that she came up here to take a job cookin' on a ranch."

"Maybe she did. Most of the cooks I've known are stove-up cowpunchers and old drunks, with a Chinaman here and there, pissin' in the bread dough. Sometimes a woman, the hard kind." He tipped his head back and forth. "If a man hires a Mexican, he might want to get more use out of her than just fryin' spuds."

"It's a world full of good ideas, isn't it?"

He shrugged. "Ideas start out like that, anyway. What did you say your name was?"

"I didn't, but it's Jimmy Clevis."

"And where do you come from?"

"Colorado."

"I see. And you got Mexican friends down there, huh?"

"I do."

He ran his fingers through his beard again. "Don't see so many of 'em up here, especially women. More in the railroad towns. You say you're lookin' fer work?"

"That's right."

"Well, they're startin' beef roundup about now. And you know where work is."

"Right. It's where you find it."

"Just like gold."

* * * * *

Farther along the trail that afternoon I talked to a freighter. He was driving a six-mule team that pulled a freight wagon with a two-wheeled camp wagon trailing behind. His load had a tarp tied down over it, so I couldn't tell what he was hauling. When I came close to his lead animals, he called out to the team and stopped his outfit. A grey-and-black dog that trotted alongside the wagon found a place in the shade and stretched out, feet forward.

I rode up even with the driver, stopped my horse, and touched my hat.

"Afternoon," the man said. "Where you headed?"

"Thinkin' of goin' to Hartville. How far is it?"

"If you camp on the Platte tonight, you should get there by mid-day tomorrow." His eyes passed over me, and he sounded dubious as he asked, "Miner?"

"Not yet. I'm lookin' for ranch work."

"Might be some north of there. If not, over on the Niobrara, the old Runnin' Water."

"That's good to know. I might go to a couple of places."

The man nodded, took out a sack of Bull Durham, and with a thick hand offered it to me.

"No, thanks," I said. As he went about rolling a cigarette, I could see he was in no hurry, and since he was headed south, I didn't worry about mentioning a little more of my business. "Do you know the ranches?"

"Some," he said, without looking up.

"I'm on the lookout for a person who was supposed to come up here and cook for one of them."

He raised his eyebrows as he licked the edge of the cigarette paper.

"Mexican woman."

He tapped the seam, lit the cigarette, and blew away a cloud of smoke. "Couldn't say."

"It's not a personal interest. She's a relative of a friend, and I said I'd keep an eye out."

The freighter brushed a couple of flecks of tobacco off his vest, then looked around at the open country. "No tellin'. All kinds of people come out here to disappear. Most of 'em want to."

"Sure seems like it."

"As for the others, everyone's got a right to go out and get lost or break a leg or freeze to death."

"I suppose."

He took in another lungful of smoke, then blew it out. "I keep to the main trails and don't go out of my way to know anything about the next fella."

"Not a bad way to be."

"He tells me his name is Bill Smith, that's good enough. He ends up feedin' the buzzards 'cause his rope was too long, that's his business too. As for a woman that run off—well, this ain't a good place to do it."

"I don't think she ran off, and she certainly didn't do it to me, but none of that matters at the moment."

He took another look around at the country and said, "It sure don't."

I looked down at the dog that was stretched out in the shade. "He looks like a good one."

"He's all right. Knows how to keep from gettin' mule-kicked, and tells me if there's any snakes in camp."

No one spoke for a long moment until I said, "Well, I suppose I'll move along. Good talkin' with you."

"You bet." He looked down his nose as he took a long drag on the cigarette and burned it back close to his beard and mustache. "Good luck to ya."

"Same to you." I touched my spurs to the little dark horse and went on my way, imagining the spirits of dead trappers, sheepherders, horse thieves, gamblers, and crib girls, all hovering over the broad country, each of them unconcerned about any of the others, much less about any live wayfarers who had not yet exercised the right to be thrown from a horse, bit by a snake, or shot through the gizzard.

* * * * *

Hartville looked like the rough town I expected. Although I had to climb to get there, it was pitched in a gulch with higher hills all around. Shadows were beginning to stretch out in mid-afternoon, and the air had a chill. People on the street, many of them workmen with red dust on their clothes and hair, just watched me as I rode by. I expected to see a saloon called the Bucket of Blood, but I settled for one that was named the Cavern.

Inside, I saw a mixture of range riders and miners, which was normal for a mining town set on the edge of cow country. I ordered a glass of beer, drank it faster than I meant to, and ordered another. From the looking-over that I got from cowboys and miners alike, I decided not to tip my hand right away even if I were to fall into a conversation. No one spoke to me, though, as I drank my second beer and took an occasional glance around.

Not knowing when I might have the next opportunity for a cooked meal, I left the Cavern after my second beer and went across the street to a café. There I ordered a steak with fried potatoes, all of which was palatable, and I took my time eating. Shadows were falling darker when I went outside, so I put up my horse in a stable and arranged to sleep in the straw for the night. After that, I went to the Cavern again.

Most of the earlier patrons had left, and a handful of new ones, cut from the same cloth, had come in. I stood at the far end of the bar and ordered another glass of beer, which I was in no hurry to drink. As I stood there, I reflected that a steak and a beer or two improved a fellow's comfort in an appreciable way, and if I hadn't been in a hard town looking for a person who was probably in trouble, I might have been content.

After a little while, a man who looked like neither a ranch hand nor a miner took a place near me at the bar. He wore working clothes but no hat, and his hair had thinned so that the top of his head looked like a smooth river rock. He gave me a half-smile as he waited for his drink. The barkeep brought him a glass of beer, and after he took a slug he tipped his head to one side and smacked his lips.

"Best part of the day," he said.

It was the kind of gesture that invited conversation, so I said, "Life's little pleasures."

"Isn't that the truth?"

I nodded.

"You must be new."

"New to here."

"Uh-huh." His glance slid over me. "Not a miner."

"Nope. Mostly ranch work."

"There's some of that." With another half-smile he said, "Me, I work in hardware."

"That's good."

"Yep. I'd rather sell picks and shovels than swing 'em."

The comment seemed like something he had delivered a few times. I answered, "Good idea."

He gave me another once-over. "I know cowboys don't care for shovels, but if you need anything else in that line, look me up. My name's Bob Underhill, and I work in the hardware store across the street."

"That's fine. I'm Jimmy Clevis." We shook, and then I said, "If I find myself in need of a crowbar, I'll look for you."

"Sure. Or a chain and a padlock." He glanced at my six-gun. "Or ammunition."

"Sometimes I think I'd like to buy a lightweight hand-ax, something to slip into the saddlebag."

"Got them, too."

I took a sip of beer. "I need to get a job first."

"Oh, yeah," he said with a quick nod.

After a few seconds, I went on in a lowered voice. "Tell me, Bob. I don't like to say someone's name out very loud, but when I was comin' up from Chugwater, a fella told me I might find work with a ranchman named Vermillion. Do you know anyone by that name?"

Bob twisted his mouth to one side. "Whoever told you that didn't know much. There's a ranch by that name, but not a rancher. The Indians used to make their dye from the red powder they found around here. That's where the name comes from."

"Oh. It could have been my mistake. Do you know where this place is?"

"Sure. You go out east past the mines, and you follow the trail through the Haystack hills. About three or four miles. The fella's name is Atwood, but I don't think he hires many men."

"Worth askin'."

Bob shrugged and took a drink of his beer. I had the feeling that he could have told me more but he didn't like to pass any comments about people who bought hammers or barbed wire in his boss's store.

At that moment, a buxom blonde woman appeared and stood between the hardware man and me. "Hello, Bob. Who's your friend?"

"This is Jimmy, lookin' for ranch work. Jimmy, this is Lil."

She smiled and said, "Liliana."

I gave her my best smile. "Pleased to meet you." I was telling the truth. Even if she looked a bit overdone, with her bubbies pushed up and almost out of her dress, and her hair tied up on top like an ornamental Chinese chicken, I got along well with women like her. She wasn't going to make me forget about Magdalena, but she was the kind of person I was comfortable talking with.

Bob took a long drink and finished his glass. "I'd better be going." Then, with a look at me, he said, "Lil can tell you more."

He pushed himself away from the bar and glided out of my sight, which was taken up by Lil's bosom as she shifted to talk to me.

"Did Bob mean something by that?"

"I don't know." With a confidential look and a lowering of my voice, I said, "I told him I was looking for a place called the Vermillion Ranch."

"Oh."

"And he didn't seem to want to say anything."

"Just as well. He had a little run-in with the hired man, who's the type that seems to look for trouble."

"I see."

She leaned forward so she could speak just above a whisper, and I got an even better view of her charms. "Keep this on the *q.t.* as far as who told it to you, but things don't seem to be on the up-and-up at that place."

"Oh." I raised my glance and met hers. "I appreciate your mentioning it."

"It's all right." She turned her head a little and gave me an arched look. "You're not going out there tonight, are you?"

"I don't plan to."

She smiled. "Then you ought to have a little time to put pleasure before business."

"Under other conditions I might not object, but I need to find some work first. Right now I couldn't afford to buy a cinch ring from Bob Underhill."

She raised her eyebrows. "Don't those things get people in trouble?"

"It's like other things. It depends on how you use 'em."

* * * * *

The trail I followed the next morning led me through red earth country, past an open-pit mine where I rested my horse for a few minutes and watched the miners moving like red ants. Then I moved on into the Haystack hills. It was rough country, full of breaks and draws with cedar and stunted pines and plenty of rocks, but I could see where an outfit could run a few cattle. The trail wound north, and after about an hour's ride beyond the mine, I found a ranch on the east side of the trail.

As I rode up to the ranch house, a young fellow stepped outside and stood waiting for me with his back to the sun and his pistol handle jutting out in a silhouette. Closer, I recognized him as one of the men who had been drinking in the Cavern when I first went there. Beneath his flat-brimmed hat he had light hair, close-set eyes, a beak nose, and ears that jugged out. He was a little under average height, with a slight build and thin-looking arms as he held his right hand near the pistol butt.

"Good mornin'," I said. "Is this the Vermillion Ranch?"

"Sure is."

I dismounted so as not to be looking down on him. "Name's Jimmy Clevis. Lookin' fer work."

"Name's Beasley."

I could see his face better now. He had a thin chin beard about a week old, set against a pale complexion that made him look as if he had just gotten out of jail. He had a smug look to him, which I pretended not to notice. "Who's in charge of hiring here?"

"Don't really need anyone right now."

"I see." I looked past him toward the ranch house. "Got a full crew?"

"Full as need be."

"Huh." I could feel my horse crowding me, so I nudged him back. "Got an idea where I might look?"

"Don't know. Haven't been lookin', myself."

The door in back of him opened, and an older man, about forty, stepped out. "Who's there, George?" he asked.

"Just someone lookin' fer work."

"Oh." The man came forward. He was wearing a brown hat and a vest of the same color, a grey shirt, and dark trousers. He had shaved within the last few days and might have had a bath in the last week, and in spite of his filmy quality I could tell he tried to maintain appearances. He smiled and gave a tug to his hat brim. "How can I help you?"

"Wonderin' where I can find some work," I said.

He smiled again. "Not much right here. The best work anywhere near is in the mines."

"I prefer ranch work."

"Sure. Who wouldn't? Thing is, though, most of that is a ways off."

"Oh? Have you got an idea where they might be hiring?"

He tipped his head to one side. "Hard to say, but a man could try up north."

"On the Niobrara?"

"That, or over by Shawnee and Lost Spring."

"I see. Well, that's good to know. Any outfits I should stay away from?"

He smiled and shook his head. "I never heard a bad word about any of 'em."

"Honest country, huh?"

"Everyone tries to be good neighbors."

"That's good. I sure appreciate the tip."

"Don't mention it. I wish you good luck."

"Thanks, Mr. —"

"Atwood. Fred Atwood. Glad to help."

"As I told your man here, my name is Jimmy Clevis." I pulled my reins out to separate them, and as no one had said anything further, I asked, "What's the best way to go from here?"

Atwood came out with the easy smile again. "Back the way you came. Go through town and out north through the gap. You'll drop down into good grass country."

"That's what I like."

"I wish I had some of it myself. But we scratch along up here with what we've got."

* * * * *

Bob Underhill cut off a piece of steak and poked it in his mouth. He wasn't shy about accepting noon dinner or about ordering a steak that nearly covered his plate, but he looked around each time before he spoke.

"Watch yourself with that fellow Beasley. He's out lookin' to prove himself, and he's a thief to boot."

"Really?"

"Yeah. He took a pistol of mine, right out of my room, and I saw him wearing it in the saloon. I knew it was mine because it has a black grip on one side and a brown grip on the other. I was on the lookout for it, and when I saw it on him, I told him I wanted it back. He told me to take it from him."

"He seems like a trouble-maker, sure enough. And he seems to be working in the right place."

Bob raised his eyes to look at me. "I'd say."

I tossed off my next question casual-like. "What kind of back-alley work are they doing out there, anyway?"

He paused with a twist to his mouth. "Are you some kind of a stock detective?"

"No, I'm just looking for a missing person. But the more I know, the more I can look out for trouble."

He shrugged, then poked his fork into a slice of fried potato.

I could tell he'd like to get George Beasley in trouble but didn't want any of it to come back on him. "I'm on my own," I said. "I don't have to report to anyone."

He raised his chin as he cut off a slice of steak. "What kind of a person are you looking for?"

"A woman. A Mexican woman who came up here supposedly to cook for this ranch, even though they don't seem to have a crew."

In a voice even lower than before, Bob said, "I think they have one, or at least they did."

My pulse picked up. "Really? At that place where I went?"

"I don't think so. They've got another place, farther back in the Haystacks."

"What do they do there?"

"Horse corrals, from what I've heard. Kind of a relay station."

I remembered hearing of a string of those places. "And they keep the woman there?"

"That's what I've heard. I saw a dark one when she first came to town. I guess they took her out there, and I haven't seen her since."

"To cook? To feed and water horses?"

Bob gave me a dead stare. "You tell me."

"Well, none of this is good."

He took a slow breath and spoke again. "I wish you were a stock detective. Get the goods on these two, and make it stick."

"I know what you mean," I said, but I didn't share his wish.

* * * * *

Back out in the Haystacks, I felt like a stock detective, dry-camping and cold-camping, moving slow, finding the high points and studying the country through a pair of binoculars. On the third day, I saw Atwood and his hired man ride through a cleft in a sandstone bluff. After two hours of working around to an even higher spot on the south, I looked down into a box canyon and saw the hideout.

No one stirred outside the cabin, but smoke was threading up from the stovepipe. The two horses the men had ridden in on were standing in one corral, while a dozen others, mostly sorrels and bays and a couple of brownish-black horses, lounged in a larger corral. As the shadows of afternoon started to reach out, I wondered if the two men were going to stay the night. If they did, I was going to have to ride down to find water for my horse before things got too dark.

I dropped halfway down the back side of the mountain and waited for a couple of hours. Then I climbed on foot, carrying my field glasses, and made another study. The whole place lay in shadow now, and no noises came up my way. Both horses were in the small corral, and smoke was still coming out of the stovepipe. Beasley stood at the back step, smoking a cigarette. From appearances, he had just fed the horses, as they were all eating.

So much for today, I thought. I needed to wait for those two to leave before I made my next move. That meant I would have to climb back up here in the morning.

* * * * *

The sun had warmed the rocks around me by the time Atwood and Beasley rode out at mid-morning. As I waited to give them time to get away, a dark-haired woman came outside and tossed a dishpan of water. Ten minutes later, I rode down the hill and around until I found the gullet leading through the sandstone.

This is it, I thought. If they've gone back in in the meanwhile, I'm in a hell of a fix. And I'm even worse off if they're not there but come back and block the exit before I get out.

I told myself I'd come that far, though, so I put spurs to Little Blackie and rode through the crack in the wall.

Coming out on the other side, I saw the cabin about a hundred yards ahead. As I approached at something of an angle, I could see past the right corner to the corrals behind. A movement flickered there, so I rode around to the back rather than pausing in front and calling out.

The dark-haired woman had finished shaking out a blanket and was draping it across the top rail of the corral where the two horses had stayed overnight. Some of the horses in the second corral had perked up and were looking my way, but the woman was absorbed in her work.

I swung down from the saddle, stepped forward, and said, "*Buenas tardes.*"

As she turned around and stared at me, I had my first real impression of what Rose of Durango was like.

She was all of thirty, if not a little more. She had a dark complexion, as Nena had said, and her face had filled in with age and had settled into a hardness, like I had seen in paintings of stoic Indians. Her dark eyes were quick and her voice was sharp as she asked, "*¿Quién eres tú?*"

"I am a friend of your cousin Magdalena," I answered, still in Spanish.

"What are you doing here?" She had a distrustful look as her eyes roved over me and my horse.

"Nena said your family was worried because they had not heard from you. Nena asked me to come see if you are in any trouble."

"I am all right." She wiped her hands on her apron, which with the charcoal-grey dress made her look more bulky than she was. "Why is Magdalena so worried? She barely knows me."

"She said your family was worried, those from Durango."

"They have so few fleas."

I had heard the expression before, and I took it to mean that her family members didn't put themselves out very much. "Well," I said, "if everything is all right, I can leave before any trouble starts."

She seemed to waver, as she didn't look straight at me.

"Tell me," I went on. "Do you want to stay here, or do you want to leave?"

She had her lips pressed together and her eyes narrowed. "I don't know."

I thought about how to re-phrase it. "Do you think you are in danger here?"

One of the horses in the corral nickered as I waited for an answer. "I don't know," she said. "They have me closed up here, and I wouldn't know how to get away, even with all these horses. But they haven't . . . hurt me." Her eyes did not hold straight as she told this last part.

"Let me ask you again. Do you want to leave?"

Now she looked straight at me. "It depends on what you want in return."

"Nothing. I'm doing this for Magdalena. They gave me some money for my expenses, and that's it. I'm not looking for anything more."

Her face was relaxed, her eyebrows half-raised. "Maybe you are like the others."

"To begin with, I don't steal horses."

A sound from the corner of the house made me turn around, and there stood Beasley with his gun drawn. He clicked back the hammer and said, "Why don't we all speak English?"

I gave a sidelong glance to the woman, and the look of contempt on her face gave me encouragement. So did her answer, in the English he asked for.

"People who don't know Spanish always think we are talking about them."

"And so?"

"Most of the time, they are not that important."

I could see his face tinge at that, but he didn't have an answer. He turned his pistol straight at me, and I pushed on my horse's reins to keep him at arm's length.

Beasley had his smug tone back. "And what about you? Do you think you're sniffin' after somethin'?"

"I don't like someone pointin' a gun at me."

"Get used to it. And you didn't answer my question."

"I'm not a stock detective, if that's what you mean."

"What I mean is, you seem to be gettin' pretty confidential here."

"What is it to you?"

"Let me tell you this much. She keeps busy enough as it is, and she doesn't need anyone else sniffin' around like a hound dog."

"You're the dog," said Rosa.

He ignored her and kept his eye on me. "I can take care of her well enough."

"You!" she sneered.

"It's what they're good for. The only mistake God made was not puttin' that dark thing on a white woman."

"You're a pig!" she seethed.

"Careful, little *chiquita*," he said, turning toward her and lifting his free hand.

"Don't touch her," I spoke out.

He waved his gun at me. "You stay put."

He took half a step in her direction, as if he was about to show who was the boss here. Then as he reached his left hand toward her, she spit at his face. That gave me the break I wanted, so I pulled my gun. He swung his around and fired, missing me by a yard, and I put a bullet through his mid-section.

He doubled over and fell on his ass, dropping the pistol in front of him.

My horse fought back on the reins, but I held on and got him under control. All the horses in the corral were jumping around and squealing, but after a moment they settled down.

Beasley didn't move. I looked at Rosa, and she looked at me.

"Let me get my things," she said.

As she went into the cabin, I picked up the six-gun. It had a black grip and a brown one. With the hammer down on a spent cartridge it didn't pose any danger, so I put it in the near saddlebag and left the flap unbuckled.

After about ten minutes she came out with a valise.

"Ready?" I asked, still in Spanish.

"Yes."

"Do you think you can ride a horse?"

23

"That's how I came here, but I'll have to put on some pants."

"Go ahead, then."

She went inside and came out again before long, wearing a pair of denim trousers and a blouse.

"How long have you been here?" I asked.

"About two months, a little more."

"Have they paid you?"

"No."

"Then I think you're justified in taking a horse." I glanced at Beasley, long gone by now. "We'll find his."

We went around front, and there was the brown horse I had seen him riding. I untied it from the hitching rail, and after helping her up into the saddle I adjusted the stirrups. Then I swung onto my own horse, and we left the hideout behind.

Now to get through the gullet. I knew it was not wide enough to turn a horse around in, so there was only one way to do it. "Let me go first," I said. "Don't get too close."

We took it at a fast walk, and everything went fine until I was ten yards from the exit. I had my six-gun drawn, and when Atwood pulled into the passageway to block it, I saw him raise a pistol and bring it around. I couldn't get a clear shot at him because of the horse's head and neck being in the way, so I shot at the ground beneath him, sending up a spray of rock chips and sand.

The animal went into a rearing fit, and I charged. The smoky-colored horse kept going up and down, stutter-stepping backward, until it reached the open. Then it went clean over with its belly up and its front legs pawing. There came a big thud, with a flop of stirrups, a scuff of saddle leather, and a groan from the rider pinned underneath. The dark horse rolled over, pulled itself up by its front feet, and trotted away from the little cloud of dust.

Atwood lay on the ground, bare-headed and smeared with dirt. His holster was empty, and I saw his pistol lying about ten feet away. His right hand rose and fell where it lay on his breastbone, but by the time I dismounted and walked over to him, the motion had ceased.

* * * * *

Rosa waited outside the hardware store as I went in to give Bob Underhill a brief account of the story. Then I handed him his pistol.

"That's it, all right," he said. "Did you get the holster from him, too?"

"I didn't have that in mind."

He turned the pistol over in his hands. "Well, I wish you'd have gotten the holster, too."

"It's still on him, and he's not going anywhere by himself. You can either go out with the sheriff or claim it when he brings 'em in."

He pushed his lips together, as if it was all a bit inconvenient.

I motioned with my head toward the window. "Is that the woman you saw before?"

He craned his neck. "I don't know. I couldn't be sure. It was six months ago."

"Six months?"

"Yeah, and one of 'em looks like another. That could be her."

I gave it a thought and said, "Good enough, then. I guess I'll be goin'. You can expect the sheriff through here tomorrow. He'll know where to go."

Outside, when I had mounted up, Rosa asked me what the man had said when he looked at her.

"It seems as if there might have been another woman before you."

"Oh, yes. A woman named Adela."

"They mentioned her?"

"Yes. They said she was dirty and greasy, and they had to get rid of her."

I bet they did. Bring in a woman from far away, and get rid of her when they wanted. "I think you were very lucky," I remarked.

She let that pass, and after a few seconds she said, "What next?"

"You can ride with me back to Colorado if you want."

"Are you still expecting a favor?"

"Not at all. I told you earlier. I'm doing this because Nena asked me to."

"That's good. Because when that boy tried something, I had to pinch his little monkey."

She didn't say anything about Atwood, and I didn't ask. I figured there was plenty to be left unsaid.

As I turned my horse into the street, I looked over my shoulder and said, "Magdalena will be happy to see you."

"Yes, and it was good of her to send you."

"That's right. She's a good girl." I adjusted my reins and set out for the long ride back. With a shrug I thought, for once in my grown life I didn't have to worry about my weakness for women. I wouldn't have minded a word of thanks, but from what I had seen on this trip, I couldn't blame Rose of Durango for keeping her distance. And besides, I wanted to get back to the arms of Magdalena.

Le Blanc Station

Del Page rested his horse for a moment on the crest of a small rise. Ahead of him about half a mile, LeBlanc Station was visible in the first grey light of morning. The place didn't consist of much. The main building was a frame structure where the original trapper post had stood. It faced south, and in back of it sat a stable and a set of corrals. Farther to the left, half a mile due north, a large rock mountain rose almost straight up. Page gave his horse a touch of the heel, and the two of them moved ahead in the stillness.

The sky lightened above the hills in the east, and the huge slabs of rock on the mountainside took on a dull shine. The lines in the surface looked like blue veins on the fat of a hanging quarter of beef.

Page slowed the horse as he approached the way station. The main building had an overhang that kept the front doorway in gloom at this time of day. Page caught a whiff of woodsmoke as he stopped the horse and swung down. Out of habit he touched the handle of his six-gun, and he was about to tie the horse to the hitching rail when the thump and scrape of an opening door broke the quiet of the morning.

A shape appeared in the doorway, and a slender, bearded man in a dark coat and narrow hat stepped into view on the wooden porch. He held a rifle. "Where'd you come from?" he asked.

"I rode in from the west."

"That road's blocked."

"Not that I noticed."

The man's eyes went from Page to the horse, where the dark stock of a rifle stood out against the grey coat of the animal. The man's eyes came back. "What's your name?"

"Page. Del Page. Who were you expecting?"

"No one."

Page let a couple of seconds pass. "I've told you my name. Maybe you can tell me yours."

"Snell."

"Do you run this place?"

"Callahan does."

Page glanced at the rifle. Judging from Snell's tenseness, he didn't think the man wanted to use the gun. "Well, I'll tell you," he said, "I'd like to turn my horse into a corral for a little while, let him rest and have a drink of water."

"Out back."

Page turned away and flicked the reins. The powdery grey horse backed up.

"Put him in the first pen," said Snell.

Page glanced at the man. "How do you like working for Callahan?"

"I don't. That is, I don't work for him."

Page led the horse around back. The sky in the east had turned scarlet, and the high wall of rock beyond the corrals showed a faint glow of pink. Page found the first pen empty, so he unsaddled his horse, left his saddle and scabbard on a hitch rack, and turned the horse into the pen. Two horses from the next corral snuffled and came close, and a lone horse from the last corral raised his head and looked across. Page spoke low to them, backed out, and slid the latch on the gate. A trough ran between the pens, and it had water, so Page left things as they were and went back around to the front door of the station.

Inside, he found Snell and another man sitting at a small, square table. A longer rectangular table a few feet away had empty chairs around it, so Page took a seat there. In the murky lamplight he made out a counter and a doorway beyond it. Sound came from the area in back—a pan on a stovetop, then a voice. A man came out and stood at the counter.

He was not wearing a hat, and he did not have an outdoor, weathered look about him. He was of middle height and average build, with straight, light-colored hair and a clean-shaven face. He had a rounded nose, a broad upper lip area, and round cheekbones, all with a light, smooth complexion and a flushed underglow.

"'Nother pot of coffee comin' up," he said.

Page saw that Snell and the other man had cups in front of them. He wondered if the three men had already finished off a pot of coffee. "Are you the proprietor?" he asked.

"I'm Callahan."

"My name's Page. I came in from the west. This man here tells me the road's blocked."

"Could be."

"Why would they have it blocked?"

"I guess they want to."

"Well, I hope they don't give me any trouble. I'm travelin' east, and I'd like to move on in a little while."

Snell spoke up. "It's blocked that way, too." He motioned at the man sitting across the table from him. "Grady and I got turned back yesterday."

Page sniffed. "From the looks of that mountain to the north, that leaves the south. How far is it to the river?"

"Less than a mile," Snell answered. "But the bridge is out. And the river's too high."

"I believe that. I crossed it at Meyers yesterday. It was high, but I didn't think it would wash out a bridge."

"It didn't," said Grady.

The man's surly tone caused Page to look at him. He was a long-faced man with drooping lower eyelids and a three-day stubble across his face. He had reddish-brown hair and a dark hat like Snell's.

Page sat back in his chair. "Sounds like I rode into a troublesome situation. I think I might want to move on as soon as I get something to eat."

"No hurry," said Callahan. "Day's young."

At that moment, a dark-haired person came out of the kitchen carrying a coffee pot. In better light, the dusky shape became a woman in a loose-fitting dress and apron. She took a coffee cup from the counter, set it on the table in front of Page, and poured it full. Steam rose from the dark surface and cleared away.

Her eyes flickered toward Callahan and back to Page. "Don't listen to him," she said. "He'll want you to help, and he's not worth it."

"Shut up, Claire."

She raised her chin, and her dark skin reflected the lamp light. "They've got you pinned down like a bug, Billy. Who do you think you can fool?"

Callahan moved a toothpick from one corner of his mouth to the other without touching it. "I don't have to fool anyone," he said.

"Well, you don't." Claire poured coffee for Snell and Grady, then Callahan, and went back to the kitchen.

No one spoke for the next several minutes. Clattering sounds came from the kitchen, and the smell of fried food drifted on the air. The prospect of a meal stirred the emptiness in Page's stomach and picked up his spirits.

Claire brought out three plates of fried potatoes and bacon. She set one down in front of Page, then took the other two to Snell and Grady. A moment later she came back with a plate for Callahan, who ate standing up at the counter.

As he caught various glimpses of the woman, Page thought there was something out of the ordinary about her. She was a good-looking woman, as nearly as he could tell with her loose dress and apron, but her posture was a little off. Her complexion didn't quite fit this part of the country, either. She was dark, but not like Mexican and Indian women Page was used to seeing. He thought she might be Cajun or Creole, a long ways from home.

After the forks had clacked on the crockery plates for a few minutes, Page spoke. "Mind if I ask a question?"

"Go ahead," said Callahan. "As you can see, people talk the way they want around here."

Page shifted his glance toward Snell. "Why did they turn you back rather than let you through?"

"They had us bring a message back to Callahan."

"I see." Page took a drink of coffee. "Are they waiting for an answer?"

Callahan's voice came up. "It's a waiting game."

Page directed his attention toward the man at the counter. "If they've got men blockin' the road on both sides of this place, I'd say they've got the advantage in numbers."

"Claire says there's six of 'em. That would be three on each end." Callahan's voice sounded matter-of-fact as he poked his fork into a slice of fried potato.

Page looked at his own plate, then back up. "I hope you don't mind, but it's in my best interests to know how things stack up."

Callahan drew his mouth downward. "Go ahead."

Page spoke to Snell again. "If you fellows don't work here, then I gather you're travelin' as well."

"We come and go, and sometimes we work out of here. We're horse buyers."

"Not for the Army?"

"We sell to a man who sells to the British."

"I've heard of that. They say about three out of ten horses actually make it into service."

"That's not our concern." Snell took in a forkful and spoke around his food. "They tell us what to look for, and we try to find 'em."

"Sure."

"They've got to be at least fifteen hands high and four years old."

"Must be a good business."

"About half the time." Snell leaned toward his plate and shoveled in another mouthful of grub.

A sound came from the counter as Callahan laid his fork on his plate. "I'm goin' to go out and feed the stock here. These folks can tell you what they wouldn't say in front of me. Do you want me to toss some hay to your horse?"

"That would be fine. Add it to my bill."

"I'll do that." Callahan put on a brown hat and went out through the kitchen.

Page turned to Snell and Grady. "Well, who are these men who've got the road blocked?"

Snell shook his head. "I don't know enough to tell you."

"I take it they know Callahan."

Grady's voice rose in a complaining tone. "He used to ride with them."

"Oh."

Claire came out of the kitchen with the coffee pot. Page assumed she had been listening, and for a second his eyes met hers. She paused at his table.

"They're right," she said. "He used to ride with 'em. But he let 'em get sent up, and he kept the loot. Now they want to settle with him."

"And he doesn't," said Grady.

Claire tossed her head. "He likes to do things his way. And he thinks he can keep on doing it."

Page frowned. "With six of them?"

Claire's dark eyes met his again. "It doesn't sound like a good idea, but that's the way he is."

"Are they trying to sweat him out, then?"

"That was their first choice, but he turned it down."

Page waved at the other two men. "Does he think we're going to take his side?"

She raised her eyebrows. "He doesn't care who he pulls into it. If it makes things more difficult, that's his way."

"Well, I don't know if that kind of idea is going to work."

Claire pushed out her lower lip and shook her head. "Neither does he." She poured coffee for Page, then for the other two men.

Page watched her figure as she went back to the kitchen. He turned to Snell and Grady, who were cleaning up their plates. "So what do you fellows plan to do, just wait?"

Grady looked up with his drooping eyes. "Might depend on what you do."

Page didn't have an answer, so he finished his meal in silence. As he was halfway through his cup of coffee, he heard the back door open. Callahan said something to Claire and came into the main room.

"Pretty nice day outside," he said as he hung his hat on a peg. "Clear sky, no wind."

Page addressed his question to the group in general. "Is there any kind of a trail over this mountain to the north?"

Callahan pushed his lips out and shook his head. "Never heard of anyone takin' it."

"I've heard there's a way," Snell said. "But you've got to be half-goat to try it. Game trails, crevices, narrow paths along the face of the rock."

"I wonder if a horse could make it."

"Not with a man on board."

Page took a sip of coffee. "Maybe a man on foot, leadin' a horse." He moved his toes inside his boot and thought of how slick the sole was.

"Lot of trouble," said Callahan.

"Just as soon have it there as here."

"You might not have to."

"Have you got a plan?" said Grady.

"The day's early. We'll see."

Page got up from his chair. "I think I'll go outside for a little while."

"You're not leavin' already, are you? I just gave your horse some hay."

"I need some fresh air and some space to think." Page laid a silver dollar on the table. "Here's this. I won't leave without telling you."

He went out the front way and around back. The saddle and scabbard were where he had left them, and the grey horse was eating loose hay on the ground. Page leaned on the top rail of the corral and gazed off to the north where the slickrock mountainside shone in the sun. He wondered how hard the going would be. Snell had said game trails. There were places a deer could go that neither a man nor a horse could make it. And if he got stuck in a place and couldn't go any farther, it would be a lot harder coming back down than going up, especially with a horse.

He heard the door from the kitchen open behind him. He turned to see Claire taking a careful step down from the doorway. She wiped her hands on her apron as she walked across the dry, broken grass.

"If you're thinkin' of how to leave," she said, "it's a good idea. Any way out of here would be. There's no need for you to get mixed up in this."

Page let his hands rest at his sides. "That's the way it seems to me. I don't run from my own troubles, but I don't like to take part in someone else's." He studied her dark eyes. "You seem to know him pretty well."

"I was married to a man who used to ride with the whole bunch of 'em."

"Did he get sent up, too?"

"No, he got shot dead."

"I'm sorry."

"So was I. But they all know it can happen that way."

"Do you work for Callahan, then?"

"I'm not his woman."

"I wasn't askin' anything that specific."

"Well, it wouldn't hurt you to know how things are."

"I suppose that's true, though I usually don't care to know any more about other people's affairs than I have to."

"He doesn't give a damn about me, and I wouldn't want him to."

"That's between you two. I don't mind you telling me, but it doesn't have anything to do with me."

"To answer your question earlier, I do work here."

"I did ask that."

"I just thought there were a couple of things it would help you to know."

Page didn't follow what seemed like a peculiar kind of repetition she came back to, but he said, "Well, I appreciate it."

"I told you the first part. The second part is that one of the men in that gang would like to have me for his own."

The comment gave him pause. "And Callahan is protecting you?"

"Puh. He'd sell me out in a minute if he thought it would save his skin. I think he's trying to decide the best way to do it."

"And I guess it goes without sayin' that you're not very fond of this other fellow."

"I should say not. Brewer's a pig. He wanted me all the time Pross was alive, and his intentions haven't gotten any better. So he's got two reasons to want Callahan dead. The rest have got only one."

"And you're telling me this so I'll have a better idea of why I should want to get clear."

"That's pretty much it."

"How about these other two, Snell and Grady?"

"They'll go whichever way the wind blows."

"Why didn't Brewer and the others let these two go through yesterday? Get 'em out of the way."

"I don't think they want anyone going for help until they've finished with Callahan."

"I doubt they'd want witnesses either, would they?"

"That's the problem. Me, they don't worry about. I've been on the inside, and I know better than to open my mouth. But these other two—I just hope they get gone before the others come for Callahan."

"You don't think he's got a chance, then."

Claire shook her head. "They gave him his choice. Either he gave himself up yesterday or they came for him today."

"Is he just bluffing?"

"He hasn't accepted those as the only two options." She motioned with her head toward the smooth, pale surface of the mountain. "You're a fool if you don't go."

"Thanks for the warning," he said. "How about yourself?"

"They'll follow me, and I can't move fast enough. But I'll take my chances. Sooner or later I'll get loose of them." She held up her hand in a small gesture of farewell. "Good luck," she said, and she walked back to the building.

Page looked into the corral to see how his horse was doing. A few dabs of hay were left. Page turned away and walked around to the front door of the station. He stepped up onto the board porch, took a look around, and went in.

At his place at the table, he saw where Callahan had left him a ten-cent piece for change. The proprietor was standing behind the counter smoking a cigarette.

"I think I'm ready to go," Page said.

"Already?"

"Nothin' to keep me here."

"You can ride with me," Callahan said. "Strength in numbers."

"I'll go my own way, thanks."

"You might want to go with me. Best way out."

"I said I'll go my own way. Alone."

"Hah. I thought maybe you'd have a little more decency when someone needed help."

"It's not my affair."

"Oh, you've been talkin' to Claire, haven't you? I know she went out there."

"What does it matter?"

"Well, she's going with me." Callahan raised his voice. "Claire!"

She came from the kitchen to the doorway and stood there without speaking.

"Why don't you tell Mr. Page to go with us?"

"Us?"

"Sure. You and me."

"I'm not going anywhere with you."

"Sure you are. You just need to convince our friend to go along."

"If he's got any sense, he'll leave on his own."

Callahan smiled. "I thought you'd like his help, especially in your condition."

Page narrowed his eyes.

"Oh, she didn't tell you? She's knocked up, you know. Oh, not me. And not the fella who'd like to get his hands on her."

Page looked at Claire, and she shrugged. "I didn't see the need to tell you that," she said, "especially when you said what you did about not needing to know about other people's affairs."

Page thought she had been a bit selective about what she said and didn't, but he left it at that.

Callahan spoke again to Page. "Just a poor pregnant widow. I thought you'd like to ride along to make sure the whole exchange goes well."

Claire's voice rose in a tone of impatience. "I'm not going anywhere with you."

"Of course you are. Go get a few things together, and I'll hitch up my horse while Mr. Page saddles his."

"I'm not going with you," she said, firm as ever.

"Neither am I," said Page.

Callahan made a small spitting sound. "Go ahead and leave," he said. "If you don't want to see her through, I'll do it myself."

Page glanced at Snell and Grady. They both sat wide-eyed with their mouths open. Page turned to Callahan, who had brushed his coat back to reveal a gun and holster.

"Look, Page. Don't be a fool. The one way any of us gets out of here is if we all go together. That's the easiest. These two said they would go if you would. If Claire goes with us, no one gets hurt."

That was it, Page thought. Callahan wanted to use Claire as a hostage or a bargaining chip. Page kept his eyes on the man. "You don't want to hand her over, do you?"

"We'll see how things go."

Page shook his head. "I don't like any of it."

"And I'm not going," said Claire. "Not with you."

Callahan's hand moved toward his gun. "I can make you."

Page moved his own hand so that his fingertips touched his holster. "Don't try it," he said.

Callahan sneered. "How are you going to stop me? You either go with us, or she and I go alone."

"Maybe no one goes anywhere."

"That's just as good. Whether we go or stay, the best is for the five of us to stay together."

Page looked at the woman.

"Go," she said. "Don't be a fool."

Page nodded. Callahan was counting on him to stay to protect the woman. Widow of one man, pregnant by another, held by a third man, and desired by a fourth. And she was the best of the bunch. Page looked at the three men in the room, and he walked out of the station.

The sun had climbed in the sky and was warming the day as he saddled the grey horse. The stock of the rifle was cool to the touch. When he had everything ready to go, he checked the loads in his pistol. Then leading the horse by the reins, he walked to the back door of the station and rapped on it.

The door opened, and Claire stood in the doorway.

"Well, I'm going," he said.

"Good luck."

"Thanks." He hesitated for a moment. "You're welcome to come along," he said.

Her face tensed. "I hadn't thought of it. Like I said be-fore, I can't move fast."

"You can walk, can't you?" His eyes roved over her loose apron and dress. "How far along are you?"

"Less than three months. I can walk all right. I just don't think I should ride a horse or do anything sudden."

Page cast a glance at the mountain. "It's all slow and on foot."

"You go," she said. "I'll remember you asked."

"All right." He put his foot in the stirrup, swung aboard, and touched his hat. "So long."

He felt a pang at leaving her to what might happen, but he didn't want to buy someone else's trouble, especially when that someone was a crook. He gigged the horse into a fast walk and rode toward the base of the mountain without look-ing back. A quarter-mile out, he turned in the saddle to glance at his back trail.

A woman was walking toward him across the flat. The white apron was gone, and she was carrying a small handbag at her side. She lifted her hand to wave, and he turned his horse and waited.

As he looked past her toward the station, he saw a horse and rider coming toward her on a lope. Dust rose, and the faint drumming of hooves carried on the air.

The horse was a sorrel with a narrow white blaze, and the rider had light-colored hair and a brown hat.

Callahan rode past her, then cut his horse around to block her way. As she turned one way and then the other, he lunged the sorrel to each side in front of her. Now he was forcing her back, trying to herd her.

Page spurred his horse and headed toward the station on a lope. He slowed as he came up close to the sorrel, then stopped as he laid his hand on the headstall.

"Leave her alone," he said.

"You stay out of this, cowboy." Callahan's voice became harsher as he said, "Claire, get back!"

Page swung down from his horse and stood between Callahan's horse and Claire. "Save your breath," he said.

"You're a meddling fool." Callahan jerked his right leg over the saddle and jumped down onto the ground.

Page assumed Callahan thought there might be gunplay and didn't want to be in the saddle if it happened.

Callahan passed the reins in back of him to his left hand, and with his right hand near his pistol butt he walked up to Page. "Get out of my way," he said.

"Leave her alone. If she wants to leave, that's up to her."

Callahan stopped. "By God, you *are* a fool."

"Don't let that trouble you."

Callahan raised his head and glanced beyond Page in Claire's direction, then brought his gaze back as he stood crowding. When Page didn't budge, Callahan's tone turned sarcastic as it had earlier, in the station. "You talk about trouble, you're settin' yourself up for plenty."

"That's for me to worry about."

"But I guess there's one good thing about it. Once they're in that condition, you can't knock 'em up again."

Page's fist came up and connected with Callahan's cheekbone, and the brown hat tumbled away. The man stepped back, regained his balance, and came at Page swinging. His right fist skidded off of Page's forearm, but his left came around and caught Page on the jaw. It didn't have much force, though, and Page didn't even lose his hat. He stepped back, got his fists up, and moved forward. He landed a right on the side of Callahan's head and sent him backward again.

Claire's voice stopped the fight. "They're coming!"

Both Page and Callahan turned to the east, where three dark riders moved toward the station on fast-walking horses. They were about a mile away.

Callahan took a couple of steps, leaned over, and picked up his hat where it fell. His hand wavered near his gun.

"You've got bigger things to worry about," said Page. "Don't make me draw."

Callahan took a deep breath and seemed to take stock of things. He walked toward his horse, which had shied back several steps. He gathered the reins, flipped them in place, and swung aboard. Turning, he said in a loud voice, "I could tell you something, but I won't." Then he kicked the sorrel in the flank and headed back to the station at a gallop.

Page got a hold of his own horse and walked to the spot where Claire stood.

"That's Billy Callahan for you," she said. "Bluff right up to the end."

Page glanced at the mountain and then at the station. "I hate to say this," he said, "but I think at this point our best chances are to go back. If you can't run, I think we'd better walk fast."

Page led the horse and kept pace with Claire. She didn't lag, but he wished she would walk a little faster. The riders were getting closer.

The sound of voices carried from the corrals, and Page looked around in time to see two dark-hatted men swing onto their horses and ride around the west end of the station. Callahan and the sorrel followed on a run.

"Snell and Grady are takin' off," Page said. "Looks like he's tryin' to stop 'em."

Claire forged ahead, and Page kept himself at her pace. When they were within a hundred yards of the station, he decided to go ahead.

"Keep walking," he said. "I'll put this horse in the corral and get right back to you." He set his reins, swung aboard, and kicked the grey horse into a lope. He rounded the corner of the corral and drew up in front of the pen he had used earlier. He swung down, knotted the reins so they wouldn't fall and drag on the ground, and pulled his rifle from the scabbard. He turned the horse into the pen and closed the gate.

Back at the corner of the corral, he waited but a few seconds as Claire caught up. The two of them headed for the back door of the main building. He couldn't see the riders from the east, so he figured they were on the other side of the station. He listened for shots, but all he heard was the sound of hooves on dry earth. In an instant, Callahan and the sorrel horse came pounding around the west end of the station. Page and Claire kept walking as Callahan jumped off the horse and pushed it into the pen.

"Get inside!" he yelled as he ran past them to the back door.

It did not budge when he heaved himself against it and tried to turn the handle.

"Damn it!" he said. "Someone's in there, and they've got it locked. Come on." He drew his gun, moved up against the building, and headed for the corner on the west end.

Page followed with Claire behind. When they heard no commotion, they went around the first corner and found Callahan a couple of yards ahead of them. He turned and frowned.

"There must be two outside and one inside. I think we've got a better chance if we get in."

Page did not like the options, but it was too late to change them. "All right," he said. Holding the rifle at waist level, he moved ahead.

Callahan paused at the next corner and waited for Page and Claire to catch up. He shifted his gun to his left hand, and with no warning he grabbed Claire by the upper arm. She backhanded him with her left hand, and with her right she swatted at him with her handbag. He let loose and grabbed again, this time at the top of her dress. Claire pulled away, and the fabric ripped. Callahan gave up on that maneuver and went around the corner by himself. Again, all was quiet.

Page and Claire followed. Ahead of them, Callahan made a break for the door. At the same moment, a man stepped out from the far corner, fired a shot, and sank back out of view.

Callahan grabbed his right thigh and slumped. Blood showed between his fingers. He took his six-gun into his left hand and limped forward. Up onto the board porch, he hobbled to the door. He passed the gun to his right hand again, and with his left he opened the door inward.

A husky man in a drab-colored, close-fitting pullover shirt appeared in the doorway and shot Callahan dead center. Callahan snapped back, landing in a limp heap on the ground, and his brown hat rolled away.

The man in the doorway swung his .45 around toward Page, who had just levered in a shell. With the stock of the rifle against his hip, Page pulled the trigger.

The man doubled over, and his pistol clattered on the boards of the porch.

Page held his arm out as he turned to Claire. "Let's get in." As they stepped up onto the porch, he said, "Who is that?"

"Pearson," she answered.

"Hold this." He handed her the rifle, then leaned over and pulled the body clear of the doorway. He straightened up and said, "Go right around him."

Page stood with his right hand on his pistol butt and let Claire go through the door ahead of him, carrying the rifle and her handbag. As she moved past, motion at the far corner of the building caught his eye. The man who had shot Callahan in the leg stepped into view. He was short, thin, and blond, wearing a wide-brimmed hat and a light-colored vest, and he had a gun pulled.

Page drew and shot him in the upper chest, and he spilled backward. Page took a quick look around. Callahan had said he thought there were two men outside, and the other one could come around a corner at any minute.

Page made it through the station door in two quick steps. Claire was standing a few feet from the door and facing it. Page took the rifle from her, set it on the table, and turned to close the door. He slammed it shut, put the steel bar in place against it, and stepped aside. He put his gun in his holster and brought his eyes to meet Claire's.

"I got the one who shot Callahan in the leg."

"That was Stovall."

Page let out a long breath and felt the tension relax in his upper body. "We might be in for a wait now."

Movement in the back of the room drew his eye. A man rose up from behind Callahan's counter and held a gun aimed past Claire at Page. He was a slender, brown-haired man of average height. He had taken his hat off, and his hair was ridged all the way around. His face was tight, as if his skin was stretched over his cheekbones, and his straggly mustache looked crooked.

"It won't be long," he said. "Claire, get out of the way."

"What do you think you're going to get?"

"We'll settle that later. Get out of the line of fire."

Claire was standing partway in front of Page and on his right. She still held her handbag, and now she shifted it to her left hand.

The other man's eyes followed her movement, then rested on her upper body where Callahan had torn her dress. He seemed to catch himself gazing, and when his face hardened again she dropped the bag and stepped to her right.

Page jumped sideways to the left and drew his gun as the other man wavered and tried to pick up his target.

Page fired twice. The first shot caught the man in the left shoulder and lifted him an inch or so as it turned him. The second shot caught him in the lower chest and dropped him.

Silence hung in the room as Page put his pistol in his holster. "That ought to be all of them for right now," he said. "Was the last one Brewer?"

"That was him."

Page listened for noises outside and didn't hear any. "The other three are probably on their way, don't you think?"

"I would imagine."

"Then I'd say we'd best get out of here while we can. How about you?"

Claire nodded. "I think I could take my chance riding a horse. You want to go the same way you were headed before?"

"It should get us out of the way." He moved to the table and picked up the rifle. "I'll get the horses ready."

He went out the back way. By the time he got his horse and Callahan's out of the pens, Claire had changed into a shirt and a pair of trousers. He helped her into the saddle, then mounted the grey horse, and they were ready to go.

They made it to the base of the mountain in short order. They dismounted, and Page went first. The path led upward through boulders for about two hundred yards, and the group came out on an open spot. Page wondered how visible they were from the station. He imagined they looked like insects crawling up the body of an unknown beast.

They went through another series of crevices, then came out and took another breather. They were a good hundred feet above the plain, and Page wondered again what they looked like from a distance. As he gazed at the station, he saw black smoke rising from it.

"Looks like it's on fire," he said.

"Sure does."

He gave her a close look. "Did you drop a match?"

She raised her eyebrows. "I might have. I was in a hurry."

He tipped back his head and gazed at the rock wall towering above them. "Long ways to go," he said.

They exchanged another glance, and with the horses in tow, they resumed their trek up the mountain.

* * * * *

Page was eating fried beefsteak in a roadhouse near Iron Mountain when a man walked up beside him and spoke in a familiar voice.

"Your name's Page, isn't it?"

He turned and looked up at a bearded face and a narrow dark hat. "Yes, it is. And your name's Snell."

"That's right." Snell held out his hand.

Page shook it. "Where's your friend Grady?"

"Oh, he'll be along." Snell paused and then said, "Well, you never know when you'll meet up again. When I saw you sitting here, I thought, I know that fella."

"Small world. By the way, how did things turn out at Le-Blanc Station that day?"

"All right for us, I suppose. Grady and I took off not too long after you did. Actually, we saddled up when Callahan went after you, and we got out of there just as he was coming back."

"I saw that."

"We went to the river and followed it out east. Rough ride, but we made it."

"How about Callahan?"

"Oh, I thought you'd heard. He and that fella Brewer both died. Them and two others. The rest of 'em lammed out of there. And someone set fire to the place. Burned to the ground."

"Too bad for Callahan. Gettin' killed, that is."

Snell gave a shrug. "Reap what you sow. At least he got some of 'em." Snell seemed to hesitate for a couple of seconds. "How about that woman Claire?"

"I put her on the train in Rock River about ten days ago."

"That was the long way around."

"We went over the mountain."

Snell raised his eyebrows. "That must have been quite a climb."

"We made it."

"Uh-huh." Snell paused again, and Page wondered if he was trying to figure out the sequence. But all he said was, "So Claire took off."

"Yeah."

"She wasn't such a bad one."

Page didn't answer.

"Did you ever find out who put the bun in her oven?"

Page raised his eyebrows. "She didn't say, and I never asked. It was none of my concern."

Snell seemed to catch the reference. "Just curious," he said.

"Lots of people are."

Chugwater Charlie

Charlie Claymore sat in the shade of his horse, reins in his lap, and stuffed tobacco into his pipe. It would have been a good moment to enjoy the quiet of the rangeland, but as often happened, the young boss had things he wanted to talk about.

"Here's the deal, Charlie. If I want to take Amy anywhere, she's got to have her old Aunt Celeste come along as chaperone. If you were the kind of friend a fella needs, you see, you'd go along on this picnic, and you could keep Auntie-Q from hangin' on every word I might want to say." George waved his hand. "Wouldn't cost you a dime. I'd pay for the vittles, the carriage, the whole shebang. And besides, it would be good for you."

Charlie watched the tobacco strands lift as he laid the match across the bowl of his pipe and drew the flame downward. "It's not a matter of money," he said. "She's not exactly my dish of prunes to begin with, and more than that, I'd just as soon not get drawn into other people's affairs."

George frowned as if he had been offended. "Affairs? This is just a matter of eatin' cold chicken and mince pie, and makin' up nice to the old lady."

Charlie puffed at his pipe and looked off in the distance, where pine and cedar trees dotted a ridge that rose up out of the grassland. It was hard to tell a young pup like George that he, Charlie, just wanted to mind his own business, stay out of trouble, and see if something good—that is, something more appealing than Aunt Celeste—might come his way. Further-more, he didn't need some youngster deciding what would be good for him, especially when the prize was, as George put it, as old as an antique. Instead of answering, Charlie shook his head.

"So you don't want to?"

"I'd rather not."

George picked at the dry grass in front of him. "How about this, then? We could have dinner at the Imperial, right where they live. Dinner for four, somethin' a little nicer than the daily meals they order there."

Charlie raised his brows as he puffed again. "I suppose I could go along with something like that."

* * * * *

The dinner took place in a small area that had been reserved and closed off from the larger dining room. Charlie took his seat across from Amy, while Aunt Celeste sat at the end to his right and George sat at the head of the table, on Charlie's left. As Charlie settled into his seat, he took in his surroundings.

The table service consisted of crystal, china, silver, and spotless cloth napkins, plus a candelabra as centerpiece. The head clerk of the hotel, a man named Craig, served as waiter. He was a thin man with straight blond hair, a pointed nose, a reddish bristle of a mustache, and a scrawny neck. He brought clear glass plates of delicacies, which George passed around—sliced oranges, sweet pickles, canned oysters on a bed of ice, and a liver paste.

For the main course, in addition to scalloped potatoes and candied yams, Craig brought a hot, crackling rib roast, which George carved as if he were the lord of the manor. Then came a bottle of champagne, with a bottle of claret soon after.

Amy took in the whole spectacle with an expression of calm appreciation. She sampled each plate that came around, ate her slice of roast beef, and drank her champagne. Her blue eyes did not rest for long on George the host and suitor, and when they did, Charlie noticed that they did not shine with adoration. Yet she did honor to the occasion, in deportment and in appearance. She wore a cornflower-blue dress with a white collar, prim and pressed, and a necklace with a small diamond pendant. In addition, she had her blond hair washed and plaited into a flawless bun, and it had a healthy shine to it.

Aunt Celeste, at her end of the table, kept to her own company, with her eyes directed downward at the morsels she sampled. Her wrinkled face gathered in a pucker as she seemed to be assessing each bite of food or sip of wine. She paid no attention to Charlie, which was fine with him, and she gave young George the same kind of appraising look as she gave the standing roast and the bottle of claret. She did not touch the champagne, and she merely lifted her left nostril when Craig took the glass away.

George poured champagne into the remaining three glasses. "Here," he said, raising his glass. "Here's to good company, and let's hope it's the first of many times like this together."

Aunt Celeste pursed her lips and closed her eyes as Amy put on a smile and said, "Thank you, Mr. Bultman. This has all been very nice."

* * * * *

Charlie and George were hanging a corral gate when a letter came from town. George read it in silence and then relayed the news to Charlie. Aunt Celeste had taken a bad fall on the staircase of the Imperial Hotel. He went on to say that the message came not from Amy but from the management of the hotel.

"Doesn't sound good," said Charlie.

"No, it doesn't. I think we'd better get into town as soon as we can."

When they arrived at the hotel, the very tone of the place told them that Aunt Celeste had died. The sheriff, fitted out with badge and pistol, was standing near the foot of the stairs and speaking in low tones to Craig, who maintained a solemn air and made slow nods of agreement.

Charlie waited in the sitting area of the front part of the hotel while George went upstairs to console Amy. From where he sat, Charlie watched the sheriff as he walked up and down the staircase a couple of times. The stairs went up a dozen steps to a landing, then doubled back to reach the second floor. From different angles the sheriff tipped his head back and studied the balustrade that went all the way around the open stairwell to form a kind of balcony. Then he went to the second floor and peered over the railings from various points along the perimeter. After that he came back to the ground floor and walked back and forth in front of the bottom stair, still looking up and around. Craig had taken position next to the newel post at the foot of the stairs, with his left arm reaching across his middle, his right elbow in his left palm, and his right thumb and forefinger jerking at his bristly mustache. From time to time the sheriff muttered as the clerk stood by, nodding at the lawman's words and gestures.

From the short distance, Charlie caught the drift of the sheriff's comments. Aunt Celeste might have died from a fall on the stairs, or she might have taken a plunge, assisted, from the second floor.

That evening, George and Charlie ate in the larger dining room, which seemed to be benefitting from a few more customers than usual. Charlie did not pass on any of the impressions he had gathered, and it did not take much to let George do most of the talking.

"Amy's shook up, that's for sure. And who wouldn't be? Even if the old lady had one foot in the grave already, it's quite a shock when she trips over her own feet and takes a dive down the stairs. Poor Amy. All alone in the world, no one to look out for her. Of course, I told her I'd do anything I could. And I think she sees the good sense in it."

"The good sense in—?"

"In havin' someone to look out for her interests, not to mention give her the sense of protection that someone like her needs."

"I see. Then you must have made some progress in your visit."

George raised his head. His wavy brown hair, neat and combed, gave him a handsome look, as did his clear blue eyes, but an almost imperceptible wag of the head, along with the next remark, made him seem presumptuous beyond belief. "Let's put it this way," he said. "I wouldn't be surprised if her pretty little hand was ladlin' the gravy for yours truly before the year's out."

* * * * *

For the next week after the funeral, Charlie felt nothing but dread. He told himself time and again it was none of his business, but he could not tolerate the idea of George taking advantage of the young woman in her state of weakness. Furthermore, he did not want to be around to see it if she allowed herself to be brought under the authority of the confident master.

On Saturday, George and Charlie rode to town and took a room at the hotel. After cleaning up, Charlie went to the saloon while George went to see Amy.

Less than an hour later, George showed up at the saloon. His face was flushed, and his blue eyes were hard and glinting.

"What-ho?" said Charlie. "Was the young lady indisposed?"

"Indisposed, my foot."

Charlie heard the little voice of caution that sometimes spoke to him. "Sorry," he said. "Somethin' wrong?"

"Wrong? I should sure as hell say there is."

Charlie gave a sympathetic nod.

George set his hat back on his head. "Give me a drink," he called.

"She threw you over, then?"

"That's a way to put it. She threw me over. More like it, she turned up her nose at everything I offered. Treated it like manure on the sole of her boot."

"Well, I'm sorry, George."

"You're sorry? I'll tell you, I wish I could be." George took the shot glass from the bartender and tossed back the drink. "I'd love to be sorry. She's just an ingrate, that's what. I offer her everything I've got, offer to protect her, look out for her—the whole thing. And she looks down her nose at it, like I came from a pig sty."

Charlie thought there might be more to it than superiority on Amy's part, but he said, "Well, that's got to go rough on a fella."

George's face clouded in anger. "What in the hell does she think? After all, what choices has she got? Where else can she go?"

Charlie shrugged.

"I'll tell you," said George, as he leveled his gaze. "She must think there's better to be had out there, but she'll find out different. And after this, I wouldn't take her as she is, even if she wanted me to. I'd take her down a peg first." He motioned for another drink.

"Well," said Charlie, "I know it's hard to take, but I think you need to let it all blow over."

"That's one way." George downed his drink. "And there's another. I'll go find a woman who won't say no." He slammed the thick-bottomed shot glass on the bar and swaggered out of the saloon.

Charlie watched as George disappeared into the night. That was another way, for sure. Charlie knew about those places. A man got what he paid for, or paid for what he got. Maybe it would make George feel better about himself. To Charlie it seemed like a low way of getting even, but he reminded himself that it was none of his business. He didn't need to have an opinion about any of it.

* * * * *

Charlie had breakfast by himself in the dining room of the hotel. George had not come in during the night, and Charlie made a conscious effort not to think about it. He allowed himself the luxury of ham and eggs, which arrived with hot biscuits and a small crockery dish of plum jam. He went about enjoying his meal.

Before he had gone very far, however, the attendant named Craig appeared at his table and set down a letter that was folded and sealed in the form of an envelope. Charlie glanced up at the man, who stood hovering with nose and mustache leaning forward.

"I'm to wait for an answer."

"Oh, all right." Charlie opened the letter, which contained a simple message:

Mr. Claymore:

Would you be willing to do me the favor of meeting with me in the sitting room of the hotel at half-past nine this morning?

                                    Sincerely yours,
                                    Amy Wilmot

Charlie raised his eyes toward Craig and said, "Tell her yes. I can do as she asks."

The man nodded and said, "I'll tell her."

                    * * * * *

Amy was seated and waiting when Charlie made his way to the sitting area in the front part of the hotel. She indicated for him to sit in an upholstered chair that sat at a right angle not far from hers.

"Thank you for meeting with me," she said.

"It's my pleasure. I hope I can be of some help to you."

Her eyes wavered and came back to him. "Maybe you can."

Charlie was prepared to fend off any requests to be a go-between with her and George, so he thought the visit might not be very long or very pleasant. All the same, he gave a reassuring smile and nodded his head.

"Mr. Claymore," she went on, "I don't want to put you in an uncomfortable position, but I don't know who else to say this to, and you seem like a trustworthy man."

He shrugged. "I try to mind my own affairs, and I try to do what I think is right."

She gave a faint smile. "That's exactly the impression I've had."

She looked at the ivory-colored gloves that she held in her lap, and then she raised her blue eyes and held them steady. "I would like to ask you to help me."

"I'd like to be able to. Of course, it depends on what it is you want me to do."

She glanced toward the reception desk, where Craig stood looking through a stack of slips of paper, and then she spoke in a lowered voice. "I have a more-than-uncomfortable feeling about everything around me," she said.

"Everything?"

"Yes. This place, the man in charge, the man who presumes to be consoling me with offers of security—everything."

Charlie gave it a moment's thought before he answered. "And is this feeling related to what happened to your aunt?"

Her eyes held steady on his again as she said, "Very closely, Mr. Claymore. Very closely."

Charlie raised his eyebrows. He thought it would have been a good time to light his pipe, especially if he were miles away and out on the rangeland, but he didn't have that leisure. If he had liked this young woman less, he would let her work to make her request, but he felt a sympathy for her, and he decided to help her along. "And what is it you would like me to do, then?"

In an even lowered voice she said, "I'm desperate to get away from here, and I'm hoping you can help me."

He took in a deep breath and let it out, slow and quiet. "I'll tell you, Miss, I usually don't like to stick my neck out, and at my age, I ought to be past getting caught up in this sort of thing." He paused and saw in her blue eyes that she hadn't lost hope in him. He went on. "But it also seems to me that a fella should never be too old or too concerned about his own situation to help someone who needs it." He thought, especially when it's a pretty girl, but he did not say that. Instead, he added, "For the sake of fairness, I think you deserve it."

"Then you might be able to do something?"

"I can try."

She took in a breath and sat up even straighter than before, as if she were about to take a leap. "Will you stand by me long enough for me to get out of this town, then?"

Charlie felt a wistful smile take shape. "I don't think I can do any less, after what I've said. And where do you want to go?"

"Cheyenne. If you can help me get that far, it's all I ask. But before you agree any further, I have to ask whether you aren't worried that this will strain things between you and Mr. Bultman."

Charlie raised his brows again. "If he has a sense of fair play, he'll let things go. And if he doesn't, then I guess there's nothin' lost that's worth keepin'."

* * * * *

George and Charlie were seated at the table in the bunkhouse that evening when Charlie told his boss what he had agreed to do.

"The hell you did!" George banged his fist on the table and made the tin plates rattle. "Why, you're the most two-faced—"

"Calm down, George. I didn't do anything to you. I just agreed to help her leave town because she didn't think she could do it by herself."

George's eyes were ablaze. "My God, you've got a lot of gall, to sit there and eat my grub and talk to me like that. You're just a low-down son of a bitch, that's what."

Charlie held up his hands. "Have it your way, George."

"Have it my way?" Specks of saliva flew as George went on. "I'm tellin' you what you are, and that's a low-down, two-faced, stab-in-the-back—"

"Look, George, she already told you it was no go."

George's cheekbones hardened. "You're right. I'm done with her. I'm talkin' about you. An ass-lickin' dog. I treated you better than any dollar-a-day cowhand ever deserved, and this is what I get for it. And you think you can just sit there and tell me about it. Well, I'll tell you what. You can just clear your stuff out of here before you do another damn thing."

"All right. That's what I'll do. I'm sorry it has to be this way."

"Sorry. For what? For nothin', that's what. Just get out of my sight. And mark my words: you're no friend of mine."

* * * * *

Sitting alone on the driver's seat of the rented carriage, Charlie handled the reins and kept the pair of bay horses headed southward. In the seat behind him, sheltered by the canopy, Amy made little sound or movement. The way Charlie had it mapped out, it would be a two-day trip. On the first night they could stay over at the station at Horse Creek, and on the next day they would roll into Cheyenne. In addition to the regular dangers of runaway horses and sudden bad weather, Charlie took into account the possibility that the resentful George Bultman might show up somewhere along the way.

At mid-day, Charlie stopped at a small creek that ran northward through the grassland. He untied his saddle horse, which had been trotting along behind the carriage all morning. After taking the horse to water, he staked it out to graze. Then he unhitched the team of bays, watered them, and set them out.

Amy, who had stepped down from the carriage when it first halted, stood by as Charlie took her trunk out of the back of the vehicle and set it in the shade on the east side. Then he lifted out the box lunch and handed it to her. She sat on the trunk while he sat on the ground to her left, with his back against the rear wheel. Having selected a sandwich for herself, she handed the pasteboard box to him.

The bread and beef, dry though they were, improved the dullness of the warm part of the day. Out of habit, Charlie scanned the countryside as he took slow bites on his sandwich.

Amy seemed to be drawn into her own thoughts, and for a quarter of an hour Charlie had the relaxed feeling that all was calm and peaceful as the broad plains stretched out around them under the mid-day sun.

In a moment the illusion was broken when a small commotion broke out among the two bay horses. Charlie pushed himself to his feet, gave a small warning frown to Amy, and walked around in front of the carriage traces. As he searched for something that might have caused the disturbance, a rider appeared among the box elder trees on the other side of the creek, a hundred yards away.

The rider sat on a dark brown horse. Both hands rested on the saddle horn, and although the man had the sun at his back so that his face lay in shadow, Charlie recognized the shape and posture of George Bultman.

Charlie tipped his head back in silent inquiry, but instead of giving any sign in return, the rider reined his horse around and trotted away.

As Charlie returned to his seat by the wheel, Amy asked if there was any trouble.

"Not exactly," he answered. "Just our friend Mr. Bultman dropping in to check on us."

"Oh, dear," she said. "I was afraid he might not leave us alone."

Charlie made a small puffing sound. "I think he's just trying to intimidate us, so it's up to us to not let him get away with it."

"I'm afraid he won't give up very easily, though."

"Oh, he's stubborn, all right. If things don't go his way, he doesn't like it. But he ought to get the idea that he hasn't got any rights or interests here."

"He might be looking to protect himself all the same."

Charlie turned to look straight at her. "Really? In what way?"

She looked at the ground in front of her. "Well, it's nothing I can say for sure, just a suspicion I have—a hunch, as you might say."

An idea began to form in Charlie's mind. "You think he might have gone too far in, um—"

"In trying to get his hands on things."

"I don't know much about it, but I wouldn't rule it out."

"From what I've seen, I certainly wouldn't."

Charlie brought out his pipe and tobacco. "Hope you don't mind."

"Not at all."

"Well," he said as he dipped the bowl of his pipe into the leather pouch, "it seems as if we're in this thing together for the time being', so if there's anything you think it would help me to know, it might not hurt to say it."

"I suppose so. It was probably foolish of me to think it could be so simple as just packing up and leaving. And the story itself is not all that secret."

"Well, you won't find me very inquisitive." Charlie began stuffing tobacco into his pipe.

"Good enough." Amy's blue eyes traveled out across the country and came back to the little camp site. "I guess it starts with money, and that being the story, it's not very long or complicated. My father died about eight years ago, and he left all his interests to my mother. She, in turn, died three years later and left everything in trust to me, with my Aunt Celeste, her older sister, as my guardian."

"I see. And where were your parents from?"

"Cedar Falls, Iowa. But my father apparently had some interests out here—land, as we understood it. Aunt Celeste thought the best thing to do would be to get the cash value out of it. But as she looked into things, she saw that some of the land was no longer in his name, and what he had hung onto did not have much value. She kept all this pretty close to her chest, though, and she let on as if we had some sizeable interests and were looking to see how we could capitalize on them."

"And you think this sparked George's interest in—"

"In my fair self."

Charlie, remembering his pipe and tobacco, brought out a match and struck it. After lighting the pipe, he said, "I wouldn't be surprised if it worked that way."

"I'm convinced of it. His only problem was that Aunt Celeste read him like a book, and she was a tough old hen when it came to him and his sweet talk."

Charlie had a clear picture of the open staircase. "And so it would have been to his advantage if something happened to her."

"Of course. But he wouldn't do it himself." Amy frowned. "Excuse me, but why are you staring like that?"

Charlie shook his head. "Sorry, Miss, but I was remember-in' how hard George pushed to try to get me to take an interest in your aunt, or at least act like I did."

Amy drew her eyebrows together. "You?"

"It was his idea, not mine. And now that I think of it, it wouldn't be beyond him to think of some way to make me look like a suspect." After a pause he said, "By golly, it could be."

Amy looked around at the open landscape. "Well, we're a fine pair now, aren't we? I'm sure he doesn't like us comparing impressions. What do you think?"

"I think the sooner we get to Cheyenne, the better."

* * * * *

Charlie held the bay horses to a brisk trot as the carriage rolled across country.

"Chugwater to the west is closer than the station on Horse Creek if we'd kept south," he said. "Not much closer, but some. We can put up in Chug for the night, then take the train south to Cheyenne tomorrow. From there it's nothin' for you to catch a train back to Iowa."

The sun had not yet touched the Laramie Mountains when Charlie turned the carriage into the main street of Chugwater.

"I've lived around here off and on," he said over his shoulder. "I know people in this place. We'll be all right."

In spite of his level of confidence, he told the man in the stable that he would like the horses grained and ready to go by eight in the morning. Then he took a casual stroll to the train station, where he learned that the southbound train would not come through until one in the afternoon. The northbound train, on the other hand, made its stop at seven-twenty in the morning. He bought two tickets for that train.

Charlie explained the change of plans to Amy. "We can take the northbound train to Wheatland, which is the next stop, and then catch the train south and get into Cheyenne the same as if we'd waited here and caught it. Meanwhile, if there's anyone on our trail, we might be able to throw 'em off."

Amy nodded. "Whatever you think is best."

"Good enough, then. We just need to be up by daylight. Get a good night's sleep if you can."

* * * * *

The calm of morning lay upon the little town of Chugwater as Charlie lugged Amy's trunk out of the hotel onto the board sidewalk. He had left his duffel bag with the rest of the gear in the stable, so the trunk was his only burden. Amy carried her handbag.

"It's a little ways to the station," he said, "but not bad." Heaving the trunk so that it would ride on his hip, he set out on a stiff walk to the station platform.

The train came to a stop with a long, slow hiss. Charlie waited to be sure the trunk got loaded into the baggage car, and then he climbed aboard to take a seat across the aisle from Amy.

In less than two hours they were in Wheatland, where they waited at the station for a little over an hour, then caught the train south. At shortly before one o'clock, they rolled into Chugwater again. Charlie watched the platform to see who got on and off, and he saw nothing irregular. The engine built up steam, and the train puffed its way out of town.

Charlie relaxed and closed his eyes as the swaying of the train and the clackety-clack of the wheels lulled his senses. Just a little longer, not three hours, and they would be inside the big station in Cheyenne. It would be pretty hard for someone to pull something there.

The sound of a door closing brought him awake. Across the aisle to his left, Amy's seat was empty. He thought she might have gotten queasy with the motion of the car, and he wondered if she had gone out either the front or the back door.

He got up, left his hat in his seat, and with irregular steps on the rolling deck he made his way to the front of the car. Inside the vestibule he opened the door to the outside, looked out, and saw nothing.

Retracing his steps, he went past his seat toward the rear of the car and paused in the vestibule there. As he reached for the latch, he heard voices. He recognized Amy's.

"Don't touch me, or I'll scream."

"You scream, and you'll be sorry."

Charlie turned the latch, pulled the door inward, and stepped forward to see Craig the hotel clerk. With his left hand, the man was reaching for Amy's arm, and with his right he held an ugly little snub-nosed .32-caliber pistol.

He swung the .32 toward Charlie, who slammed down with his closed fist on Craig's wrist. The gun clattered on the landing and fell to the roadbed that went fleeting below.

Craig, who had bent forward with the blow, straightened up and clawed at Charlie's bandanna. Charlie tried to punch but felt himself being hauled forward. Craig was stronger than he looked, and he swung Charlie into the railing at the edge of the landing. Charlie broke free and got in a punch that skidded off the other man's cheekbone. Craig closed in and grabbed the waist of Charlie's trousers, and Charlie knew it was now a matter of one or the other of them going over the edge. With his open left hand he grabbed the man's sinewy neck and slammed him against the end wall of the car. Craig pushed back, so Charlie grabbed the man's shirt and used the momentum to hurl him over the railing and into the space between the two cars. As the racket of the train took over, Charlie felt the tailwind ruffle his hair.

He turned to Amy. "Are you all right?"

"I think so."

"Where did he come from?"

"I don't know. I had begun to doze off, just as you did, and I woke up with his pistol pointed at me. He forced me out here, and I think he wanted to push me over rather than put a bullet hole in me, or he would have done something right away. He kept grabbing at me, and I kept pulling away. Thank God you got here when you did."

"Thank God is right." Charlie heaved a breath and said, "Let's go back to our seats." As he opened the door of the car, there in the vestibule stood George Bultman with his thumb resting on the handle of his six-gun.

"Just step right back, Charlie. Stand over there by Missy." With an air of full authority, George moved forward and pulled the door closed behind him.

As he did so, he went to pull his six-gun from its holster. With his right hand on the pistol grip and his left hand on the door handle, he left himself open for a second. Charlie drove his solid right fist into the man's stomach and then crossed with a left on his jaw. As George staggered against the door, Charlie pulled the man's six-gun and held it on him.

"I think you know what you're up against now, George. And don't think I'd hesitate to keep you from doing any more."

"You're brave now, aren't you? You've got the girl for an audience."

Charlie eared back the hammer. "For a witness, you mean."

"Witness of what?"

"Of what you and your man Craig just tried."

George tossed his head back. "You make me laugh. You're nothin' but a pot-licker. If you ever shot a tin can in your life, I'd be surprised."

At that moment the train gave a dip and a lurch. It must have been what George was waiting for. As soon as things went out of level and Charlie was shifting position, George made a grab for the gun. He closed his hand around Charlie's but only well enough to cause him to pull the trigger.

George fell back against the side railing, his hand pressing his shirt where blood was seeping through. With a final blaze in his eye he lunged toward Charlie, who stepped aside and let him stumble and slump to the floor of the landing.

Charlie looked down at his former boss. "I'd say I'm sorry, George, but every time I said it before, you mocked me."

* * * * *

Beneath the high ceiling of the train station in Cheyenne, Charlie took leave of Amy Wilmot. "I hope things go well for you when you get back among your people," he said.

"And I hope everything goes well for you. I'm afraid you don't have much to go back to."

"Not much less than I had before this business came along. I've got my horse, and I can go back to what I know, which is bein' a ranch hand."

She hesitated, moistening her lips. "It's a great understatement to say that I'll never forget how you went out of your way to help me."

Charlie felt a tightening in his throat. "Knowin' you'll remember, it'll be a pleasure to reflect on."

"And that's all you're left with."

"Oh, it's good enough."

Her eyes softened as she seemed to see him in a new way. "You'll spend the rest of your life alone."

Charlie smiled. "Don't worry about me. There might be someone out there yet, and knowin' that you'd want me to be happy might give me the nerve I need."

A tear started in each eye, and she laughed them away. Then she kissed him on the cheek and said, "There's for nerve, and I can't imagine you not having it when you need it."

For the Love of Camille

She came into my saddle shop for the first time, and what I imagined would be the last, on a bright spring morning. I didn't get many female customers to begin with, and I wouldn't have expected Camille Morgan. But there she was, closing the door behind her as the bell tinkled.

I walked over to stand behind the counter, where I placed my hands on the leather mat that served as a meeting ground for me and my customers.

She looked pretty, as always, with her blue eyes and blonde curls. She wore a light summer hat and a pale yellow dress, and she carried an air of freshness about her. All the same, she had worry on her face as she held her handbag with both hands.

"Sammy," she said, "can I ask you to do me a favor?"

"Depends on what it is, but probably so."

She put her handbag on the leather mat. "I want you to be my postman," she said.

"Your postman?"

"Yes—or my post office." She glanced back at the door, then said, "Can I leave a letter with you?"

"A letter for someone else to pick up?"

"Yes."

I thought for a second. I knew she was supposed to be marrying George Belshaw in the fall, and I imagined the letter was not for him. The general talk around town was that her family had pressured her into marrying Belshaw because he had money and a big ranch, which would be a good connection for her family. From what I knew of her, I believed that her family would have had to pressure her. Belshaw was older, past thirty, and he did things with method and authority. Camille acted more out of impulse. If she didn't want to marry him, I sympathized with her. As far as that went, even if she did want to marry him, I hoped she wouldn't. So I said, "Well, all right."

Her face relaxed, and the tension seemed to disappear from her shoulders and arms. "I knew you would help me, Sammy. You're such a sweetheart." She reached into her handbag and took out a slim, cream-colored envelope. It looked as important as a gun and as delicate as a perfumed handkerchief. She laid it on the leather mat between us.

I turned it over. It had nothing written on it, so I said, "Do I need to know who it's for?"

"No, you don't need to know his name. You'll know him when you see him. He'll ask for it."

"Well, I don't suppose very many people will come in here asking for mail."

"I hope not."

I slipped the envelope under the mat. It was a flat, heavy piece of leather, about two feet square and more than a quarter inch thick. Putting the envelope under it was like tossing a rock into a pond—the letter just disappeared. I closed my left eyelid in a reassuring wink as I ran my right thumb and forefinger across my lips.

"Thank you, Sammy." She looked over her shoulder and then back at me. "I think I'd better leave. I never know if someone's watching me." She took her handbag off the counter, and as she was turning to go, she stopped and turned back halfway. "Thank you, Sammy," she said again. "You've always been a sweetheart." She had a beaming smile then, and I knew it was put there by someone I was yet to meet.

"It's all right," I said. I wanted to ask, "Why couldn't it be me?" But I had learned long ago that such a question would make no sense to her.

* * * * *

There had been a time when I adored her, back when I used to work on her father's ranch. I was a bunkhouse cowhand, and she was the boss's daughter. I used to saddle her horse for her, and if she went on a ride by herself, in spite of her parents' warnings, I would follow at a distance. When she got back, I would comb and curry the little roan horse. I always made sure he had feed and water, and I saw to it that he had a dry stall in bad weather. If there was anything else I could do, I did it—but all in the line of duty as a trusty hired man. If she wanted a bucket of chokecherries, I went out and picked them. If she wanted a kitty cat, I went to town and fetched it home in a gunny sack.

She knew I loved her, but she pretended not to see it. After all, I was just a poor boy, working for a dollar and a dime a day. I knew my devotion was hopeless, but I couldn't make myself feel any different.

My hopelessness came to an end, but not all at once. One rainy day in September, a horse slipped on a slick spot and landed on my right leg. That was the end of riding for a living, the end of my punching cattle for the Morgan ranch. I moved into town, borrowed money here and there, and bought the saddle shop.

I had been in the shop for two years, and I had gotten used to the idea that it was my life now. I no longer spent my days on horseback and in cow camps. I spent them within four walls, in a little shop full of leather and rope and metal—saddles and bridles, lariats and hemp ropes, bits and spurs. It was honest work, and I learned to do it. It gave me a sense of worth, something I didn't have when I was a poor boy in love with the boss's daughter.

I would see men come striding in on two good legs, just as I once did. Although I couldn't ride like I used to, I liked to think I was of some use to those who could. I also thought that in a way, I was freer than I used to be, because my life was my own.

I stood at the counter for a long moment after she closed the door behind her. So she wanted me to be her postman—me, the loyal servant after all. I supposed I hadn't changed to her, just to me. Well, I had said I would.

* * * * *

I didn't have to wait very long until someone came calling. The next afternoon, a husky cowpuncher came into the shop. He was dressed in clean range clothes, and he was neatly combed and shaved. He had a sturdy build, so his vest fit him tight. He had brown hair, blue eyes, sunburned cheeks, and solid features to his face.

He came walking up to the counter with a sense of purpose about him. I rested my hands on the mat and asked how I could help him.

"I was wondering if you had something for me."

"Your name?"

He seemed to hesitate, and then he said, "Trilling."

"Was it something you left off?" I asked.

"No, it was something I was supposed to pick up. But I don't think my name was on it."

It didn't take me long to study him, because he didn't give much to observe. His face was hard like a stone wall, and it didn't show any inspiration. Something told me he was not the right man.

"I don't know what that might be," I said.

His head moved down and up in a short motion. "Thanks," he said, and he left.

That evening, just before my closing time, another cowpuncher came into my shop. The stubble on his face and the wrinkles on his clothes made him look as if he had just ridden in from the range. His hat was tipped back, showing sandy-colored hair that fell onto his forehead. His blue eyes sparkled, and his face had a glow that didn't come from punching cattle. He walked with a free and easy gait, with his chaps swishing and his spurs jingling.

"Do you have something for me?" he asked, with a smile.

I knew he was the right man. "What does it rhyme with?"

"*Better*," he answered, and his smile broadened.

"From?"

He paused for a few seconds and then, with his eyes twinkling, he said, "Rhymes with *reveal*."

"Do you know Trilling?" I asked, wondering if the first man had given this man's name.

"Sure. He works for Belshaw."

"Do you work there, too?"

"No, I work for Frank Morgan."

"Why don't I know you boys?"

"We both hired on this season, just a little over a month ago."

"Oh. Does the boss have you out on the range now?"

"He tries to keep us there." The young man was still smiling, and I could see he had faith in young love, even as others tried to work against it.

"Well," I said, "let's see." I lifted the leather mat, pulled out the letter, and set it in front of him. It looked dainty and out of place in a shop full of leather and ropes and shiny metal.

"Thanks," he said, folding it and tucking it into his trousers pocket. His face was still glowing as he nodded to me and turned away. His spurs jingled as he walked to the door, and then the bell tinkled, and my shop was quiet.

* * * * *

In the café at noon the next day, I heard the news. Frank Morgan's daughter had run off in the night with a cowboy he had fired for coming into town. There was lots of talk one way and the other, about how much a man should try to control his daughter's life, and whether young people should run off like that.

I kept my comments to myself as I ate my dinner. I didn't think Camille and her champion had chosen a good way to start out life together, but I had seen the look on both their faces. I thought they at least deserved a chance to find out whether it was going to work. As for my part in it, I thought that if these two people were really in love, the least I could do was help.

* * * * *

The next time I saw Camille Morgan, or Camille Lashley as she was now called, was five years later. She came into my shop as before, but not in a misty cloud of young love. She had a worn look about her, maybe a drier texture and a general hardening of her features, and I thought I saw a trace of worry in her eyes.

"Good afternoon, Sammy."

"And a good one to you. Long time, no see."

She was wearing a dark blue dress and jacket with a wide-brimmed hat of a lighter blue. It was a nice outfit, and I recognized it from several years before. Her gloved hands adjusted their grip on her handbag as her eyes brushed over me. "The years have treated you well."

"You look fine, too," I said. She had kept her figure, even after having two children, and her hair was still shoulder-length and clean.

"I'm all right." She glanced up and around and came back to me. "You did me a favor once, Sammy."

I shrugged. "You asked me to."

She took a long breath, as if she needed to work herself up to something. "Well, today I'm going to ask you to do another."

My heart was in my throat. I had the terrible fear that she was going to ask to borrow money, and I didn't know what answer I could give. I tried to keep myself steady as I said, "Always depends, but I'll do what I can."

"It's about Will. You know him."

"I've barely met him, but I've seen him around since the two of you came back." As I pictured him, I saw him sitting at a card table. Like other men, he was known for getting into long games of Pedro and pinochle—nothing as ruinous as the high-stakes and quick-money games, but an expense of time at the very least, and it gave a man a reputation.

"I thought things would be better," she said. "I didn't expect Daddy to take him right in, but I thought someone would give him a break." She shook her head. "But they won't."

From what I had heard, the fellow never lasted more than a season at any ranch he had worked on. And his habits in between jobs kept his family living pretty close to the green. "It's hard," I said. Easy words, but something to say.

"He should be a foreman."

I'm sure my face fell. I didn't know what to say in return, and I had no idea of what I could do to help him get where she thought, or at least said she thought, he should be.

"He knows all about cattle," she went on. "And horses. And how to run men. He's got a thousand good ideas and could really help an outfit if they would only give him a chance."

"Uh-huh."

"He's been at this work for ten years. He's worked upper ranges as well as grass country. On top of knowing everything about horses and cattle, he can fix windmills, put up hay, even do a little blacksmithing."

"He ought to do all right."

"Of course he should. But no one wants to cross Daddy."

"You think that's it."

"A good part of it. And I think some people just don't want to give a chance to someone who knows more than they do."

I had the impression that I was hearing things she had heard from her husband a hundred times over. I wondered if she really believed it all or if she had just convinced herself. But I still had a soft spot for her, and I didn't want to make it too difficult for her to ask the favor. I said, "I don't know what I can do."

She looked past me and came back. "Someone new has bought the Double T."

"I heard that."

"A man named Morton. And Will has put in to be the foreman."

"Oh."

"He needs references, Sammy."

I frowned. "And you think I'd be any good?" As soon as I said it, I realized there weren't many men that either he or she could ask.

"You've been here a while. People have a good opinion of you."

"But I don't count for anything. And I barely know him."

"I've told you all about him, Sammy. He can do the job as well as anyone. And better."

My eyes met hers, and I thought she would always remember me for this, one way or the other. "All right," I said. "I'll do what I can."

Her face relaxed, but not as much as I might have wished. "Thank you, Sammy. I knew I could count on you." She reached her gloved hand across my counter and touched mine for an instant. Then she withdrew and said, "I need to be going. Thank you again."

I rested my hands on the leather mat as I watched her walk to the door. This was the way it was, I thought. The other fellow got the girl he wanted, and now he took her for granted, just as she took me. At least she didn't call me a sweetheart this time.

When she opened the door, a rush of cold air came in. It brought me back to the moment. A foreman job would give him work through the winter.

* * * * *

A cold, bitter wind came out of the northwest, and the sky was grey. I had lit a fire in my little pot-bellied stove and was mending the britching for a packsaddle when a stranger came into my shop.

He was an older man, about fifty, with a dark bushy mustache and a full face. He wore a brown wool coat and a dark blue, short-brimmed hat with a crease down the middle of the crown. Right away I connected him with Camille's visit a couple of days earlier.

As soon as the doorbell went quiet, I said, "Good day."

"How do you do." He made a motion as if to take off his hat, then settled it back on his head.

"What can I do for you today?"

His face became firm, and then he spoke. "My name's Morton. Paul Morton. I've bought the Double-T, out east of here."

He didn't make a motion toward shaking hands, so I rested mine on the mat and said, "Welcome to the area. I hope you like it here."

"I'm sure I will." His glance flitted around the shop and came back to me. "Been here a while, I guess."

"I've had this shop for about seven years. Did ranch work before that."

"Takes patience to do this kind of work."

"At times."

"Looks like you've stuck with it."

"I've done all right."

He breathed in through his nose, a heavy sound, as if he was working on his own patience. I could tell that small talk wasn't his strong suit.

His chest went down as he exhaled. "I understand you can give a reference for Will Lashley."

"I believe so."

"Known him long?"

"I first met him about five years ago."

"Then you haven't worked with him or for him."

"No, I had the shop by then."

"And he hasn't worked for you."

"Oh, no. I've got no land or cattle."

"I thought maybe he'd trained a horse for you or somethin' like that."

"I don't ride as much as I used to. You see, I broke my leg."

"Oh, I'm sorry—"

"That's all right. It's how I ended up here. I've got no complaints."

"Sure. Well, back on the subject of this Lashley fellow, what can you tell me?"

I shrugged. "Friendly sort. I think he gets along with others pretty well. From what I've heard, he knows his work. Certainly more than I ever knew about it. He's been at it longer."

"Would you work under him if you still did that kind of work?"

I had gotten so used to the idea of never riding again for a living that the picture didn't seem very real to me. "I suppose," I said.

"Would you hire him if you were in my position?"

I was struck by what an impossible question it was. Would I hire a fellow who loafed around saloons and card rooms? Would I want to be the one to decide whether Camille's husband had a job or not? For the love I once had for Camille, I lied. "Sure," I said, with a smile. "But I have a hard time imagining ever being in that position."

"Well, when you are, you don't like to make mistakes."

"Oh, I've seen enough to know that."

He smiled for the one and only time. "Well, thanks," he said. "If I ever need any leather work, I know where to come." He glanced around the shop again.

"I'm always here."

He turned and walked to the door, pushed his hat down onto his head, and went out into the cold wind.

So much for that effort, I thought. I had done what I said I would. Camille had done what she could, and I had sympathy for her. I should have felt free of the problem, but a question still nagged at me.

* * * * *

Later that day I rode into the wind myself. I could still ride, but not hard and fast, and the lower part of my right leg always hurt after about a mile. The place I rode to was four miles west of town, and on this day I rode the horse I usually rented from the livery stable. He was a bay about fifteen years old, and he knew the way as well as I did.

I tied up at the road ranch as dusk was falling. When I went inside, the lamps were lit and Fred the swamper was building a fire in the sheet-iron stove. He called through the curtain as I took a place at the bar.

In less than a minute, Louise came out and stood behind the bar. Her eyelids drooped like always, and her face was heavy and flushed.

"Regular," I said.

She poured me a mug of beer, set it in front of me, and walked down the bar to stand by herself.

Out of the corner of my eye, I saw another woman come through the curtain. I turned, and the sight of her made me smile. Her dark hair fell below her shoulders, and her bosom nearly spilled out of the top of her low-cut dress.

"Hello, Shawnee."

"Hey there, Sammy." She sidled up next to me and put her hand on my forearm. "Did you come to see me?"

"I don't know," I said. "Mostly I wanted to get out of town for a little while."

"Well, this is the place." She pursed her lips. "You look serious today."

"Maybe I am."

"We can always take care of that." She nudged me, and when I didn't do anything in return, she said, "What's the matter, Sammy? Has something got you down?"

"Nothing to keep me that way. Just got me wonderin'. It's about someone I know. Or used to know."

"Some girl."

"Used to be. She's married now, has kids."

"Sure. They all do that. Or a lot of 'em do. But you shouldn't let it get you down."

"I don't think I do. Like I said, I just wonder."

"Well, let's hear it."

"You don't mind?"

"No, go ahead. Lay it out."

"Well, here's my question, then." I took a drink of my beer and stared at the two of us in the mirror. "If a woman marries a fellow and he turns out to be a dud, she pretty much has to stick up for him anyway, doesn't she?"

"I think so. She made her bed, and she should lie in it."

"Does she kid herself about it?"

Shawnee's eyes met mine in the mirror. "I don't know about that. From the ones I've seen, the women who seem to kid themselves about their husbands usually know better and are just puttin' up a good front."

"Why would they do that?"

"It's the better of two bad choices. What would she look like if she admitted the truth outright?"

I wondered if it could be that simple. I said, "Do you think she tries to make him look better because she still loves him?"

Shawnee shook her head as she held me in the mirror. "Don't ask me, honey. I don't know a thing about love."

"Sometimes it seems like throwing good money after bad, but I imagine even the bad seems good at the time."

"Sure it does. And there's no sense of you wearing your-self out about someone else's trouble."

"You're right," I said. "It's between them. I need to go back to what I knew before. Just stay clear of it. Know noth-ing." But even as I said it, I was pretty sure I had my answer.

Camille was no fool. There was just no accounting for love, that was all.

Where the Water Once Ran

As Pete Wakefield rode toward the cabin, he could see signs of a dry winter. The brittle grass that crunched beneath the horse's hooves should have more green coming up through it. The country had gotten drier and drier as he rode the five miles up from the river, but now that he was on his own land, he noticed the dryness even more.

At the cabin he swung down from the saddle and stared at the windowless front wall. The door still hung in place, at least. Pete was in no hurry to look inside and see what rats and mice could do in two years. He had a good enough idea for the moment. A dugout was liveable, even snug in the winter, but a fellow was burrowed into the hillside like an animal all the same, and it hadn't been much to leave behind. He couldn't have any complaint about rodents moving in.

He pulled all his gear from the horse, and leading the sorrel by the reins, he walked the hundred yards to the dry streambed. A few spare bushes, leafless still in the time between winter and spring, lined the bank. Pete walked to the edge and peered at the arid bottom, where a rock here and there rose through the carpet of wind-blown debris. It gave him a tight feeling in the center of his body to see what he knew he was going to see—this place where the water once ran.

Back at his campsite in front of the cabin, he took a drink from his canvas water bag. He'd have to go easy on the water.

He had a long way to haul it. Save some for the horse, some for coffee in the morning. He looked at the drab sky. No telling how long till rain might come.

He rubbed down the sorrel and picketed him on the short, dry grass. The horse hadn't sweated much, but he was going to get thirsty all the same. It would take a smart jackrabbit to get any moisture out of this prairie.

Damned if it didn't look like Gilman coming over the rise. Huh. Sure was. Same old Ed Gilman.

The rider came in at a trot, swung down a few yards out, and led the horse as he walked the rest of the way. "Come back to look at things?" he called out.

Pete saw the Bar-D brand on the horse's hip. "Wouldn't take long."

"Where you been?"

"Other places."

"Surprised you came back."

Pete shrugged. "My place." He turned half around and then back. "Looks like someone did away with my corral."

"Couple of hands holed up here the first winter you were gone. I believe they used it for firewood."

"Pretty clean about it. Burned every stick, it looks like. Doesn't take that much to heat a little dugout like this one."

"I believe they had their fires outside."

Pete turned to see the hole in the wall where the stovepipe had crooked out. "Someone took the stove, huh?"

"Must have." Gilman gave him a close look. "Does that bother you?"

"Looks like I'll have to get another one."

"What for?"

Pete stared at him. "To make coffee. Fry bacon. What do you think?"

"Oh, then you're not just stayin' over for a day or two."

"I guess not."

"What the hell you want to do somethin' like that for? I thought you left."

Pete shrugged as before. "My place. I decided I wanted to live on my own land again, so I wouldn't feel so poor in my blood. Get my feet on the ground."

Gilman shook his head. "I don't know what for. You couldn't live off a hunnerd and sixty acres even if you had water." He wrinkled his nose. "It's really not worth the trouble."

Pete glanced at the Bar-D brand again. "You've been workin' for Dorrance, huh?"

"Work's work. Don't take it personal."

"No need to." Pete gazed at the horse's hooves for a few seconds, then looked up. "But now that I'm back, I wouldn't want him to run any of his cattle on my place. I'll fix the places where the fence has been cut, and I hope that works."

Gilman looked around at the dry grassland. "It's a hard go." He checked his cinch, said, "Good to see you again," and swung onto his horse.

"Good to see you, too."

Little puffs of dust rose from the shortgrass as Gilman rode away. It was a hard go, all right. None of this had much value, but even the round, smooth rocks in the dry streambed made it seem worth coming back to.

* * * * *

Pete was standing in the street, tying the sorrel to a hitching rail, when a flash of blonde hair and a familiar contour caught his eye. She had walked right past him.

He stepped up onto the sidewalk and called, "Annie," not very loud.

She turned and waited as he walked toward her. Her face showed uneasiness, pain. "You're back. Why did you come?"

"Because I didn't like the way I left."

"It was the best thing you could have done. The next best would have been not to come back."

"Well, I did it anyway. And there's no reason to act like you don't know me. I know you're married to him. I don't want any part of any of it."

Her blue eyes looked cold and hard. "Then why did you come back?"

"I told you. I had to square things with myself, not anyone else."

"I wish you hadn't."

"I've got a right to, and I've got somewhere to live. I don't owe anyone anything."

Her face softened. "Pete, you can't make a living there. You've told me that yourself."

He felt himself tighten. "Maybe I can't, especially at first, but living on my own place makes me feel as if I'm worth something." He saw the hopeless look on her face and then added, "It's not the value of the land but coming back to what's mine and living with that. Not letting anyone get to me."

"Even if you're a stone in someone's shoe?"

He shrugged. "I can't turn around and leave again just because someone else would feel better with me gone."

"You did before."

He took a measured breath. "I left because I felt I'd had my nose rubbed in the dirt. And I came back so I wouldn't stay gone for the same reason."

She shook her head. "I don't want any trouble."

"And you think I could be some. Well, I've got no quarrel with you, or anyone else, just as long as no one brings it to me."

"Is that your way of asking me to carry a message?"

"Oh, no. Things should be already understood. You knew I was back, didn't you?"

She twitched. "Yes."

"Then he's already heard what little I might have had to say."

"You can be a hard man sometimes, Pete. I liked you when you weren't."

"Not always. But that's all right, too."

* * * * *

Pete sat in front of the cabin, greasing his new cast-iron skillet. The sooner he put in a stove, the less time he would have to spend roaming for firewood. Even with two canvas bags, he still had to go to the river at least once a day, and if he could drag back enough firewood in one trip, he had more time to clean out mouse nests, plug holes, and pick up trash that the squatters had strewn around. Then move on to the next thing. He didn't know how soon he could rebuild the corral, or where he might find work to pay for the repairs.

Here came Ed Gilman again, probably with more words of encouragement. Pete set the skillet on a smooth rock about as big around as a loaf of sheepherder's bread. One good thing to come from the dry wash, water or none.

He stood up and waited as Gilman rode in and dismounted.

"Afternoon, Ed."

"Afternoon." The rider glanced in the direction of the shiny frying pan, then at the two canvas water bags hanging on the hitching rail. "Gettin' settled in?"

"Somewhat."

Gilman cleared his throat, then drew a cloth sack from his vest pocket and went about troughing a paper and shaking tobacco into it. Without looking straight at Pete, he said, "I know you don't want my advice, but I came over here on my own to give it to you."

"No harm."

The other man pulled the string with his teeth, offered the bag, then slipped it into his pocket. He rolled the cigarette, licked the paper, tapped the seam, and held the finished product between thumb and finger. "You'd just as well not get too dug in here. No one's happy with you back."

"You think I should leave."

Gilman raised his eyebrows, wagged his head, then flipped the cigarette into his mouth and lit it. "Might as well. You got no water. What good is this place to you? Especially after this dry winter we just had."

"Damn you, Ed, you don't have to be that way. Here I am sittin' on my quarter section with my fences cut, and cow manure all over where someone grazed a herd across here, and you act like I'm just in the way."

"I didn't cut no fences. Not yours."

"Well, someone did, and someone drove the cattle here."

"Orders is orders. Don't matter too much who did it."

"If it's good enough for someone else to graze on, then I imagine it's good enough for me."

Gilman blew a lungful of smoke up into the air. "What good is fenced pasture without water? What few cows you could run on this piece wouldn't have a drop to drink."

Pete flared. "You know damn well why I put the fence here to begin with. Everybody did—everyone who took up land along water. And I've got my doubts how the stream changed its course and followed the other fork, though I can't prove it now. I saw it before I left, where the channel was dug out and the mud piled up, but I was leavin' then, and I said to hell with it. Now it looks all normal, and not likely to change back, but I don't like to be mocked for it."

"I'm not. I'm just sayin' that the way things are, this pasture can't do you much good. And besides, I wasn't even workin' for him then."

"I know."

"You can be pretty damn hard-headed, Pete."

99

"I know that, too. But no one else'll do it for me."

* * * * *

Pete ordered a glass of beer. He knew his money wasn't going to hold out forever, but damned if he was going to live like a badger all the time. He could get a job soon enough, and in the meanwhile it felt good to have had a barber's shave and a bath. Now this. He slid a five-dollar gold piece to the bartender and took a sip.

He drank the beer and a second one, trying to pace himself and make the pleasure last. The saloon began to fill up, at the card tables as well as along the bar. A cowpuncher on his left said, "There's some titties."

Pete looked past the puncher and saw a saloon girl with dark brown hair cascading over her shoulders onto an ample bosom. "You like her?"

The puncher shook his head. "Can't afford it. She costs twice what the others do, says it's because she's twice as good."

"Maybe she is. Did she just get here?"

"Yeah. They come in every night at this time."

"That's the time to get her, then, before anyone else does. Her price doesn't go down as the evening wears on, I'm sure."

"Not at all."

Pete clinked his silver dollars on the bar top. "If a man was going to, now would be the time."

"All yours, if you wanta pay for it."

Pete set the coins in a neat stack, then gathered them in his hand. "If that's what it takes to get wet right now, I guess I can give it a try." As he pushed away from the bar and stepped toward her, the woman in the dark hair smiled.

* * * * *

Pete rolled out of his blankets in the livery stable. His little holiday was over, he reckoned, and it was time to get back to business. Find some work, sack away what he could. Don't cry about what he had just squandered. He could make it back in a week; he just had to find a job. Outfits would be putting on hands pretty soon for spring roundup.

As he led his horse out onto the street, three riders came pounding in from the river. They made quite a bit of commotion in front of the café as men came out onto the sidewalk.

"Lookin' for a damn kid!" shouted one of the riders.

"What kid?" came a voice from the crowd.

"Damn long-haired kid. Caught two of 'em puttin' a rope on a calf, chased 'em to the river. Both of 'em went over in the current. One of 'em drowned for sure, the other one swam free." The rider was breathing hard as he shouted his story.

Pete took in the brands on the horses, all Bar-D. Too bad for the kids, either or both.

"How about the horses?" came a voice.

"The one that the kid got tangled up in, it probably went under. Looked like the other one might have gotten free, farther down."

"So there's a kid on foot?"

"I think so, 'less he found his horse. Like to catch the little son of a bitch, show him what's what."

All three riders, still mounted, milled for a few seconds and then hit a lope east out of town. Pete followed at a walk, and their dust had long settled when he came to the ford where he got his water.

He let the sorrel drink, then filled the canvas bags and hoisted them onto the saddle. As he looked around in the deadfall for a likely branch to drag home, his glance lighted on a dark form in the thicket. He went for his saddle gun and pulled it from the scabbard.

Levering in a shell, he called over. "Come on out of there, and step light."

A minute later, a wincing kid of about seventeen, hatless in straggly hair, came into the open leading a horse. The boy was shivering in his wet clothes, and the horse gave a big round shake that rattled the leather and jingled the bits.

"Lose your pal?"

The kid nodded.

"Sorry to hear that. You've got some Dorrance riders madder'n hell at you, and I don't envy you for that, either. But if you want to come along, we can make a fire at my place and get you dried out. Let's find some wood to drag back. I see you still got your rope."

* * * * *

Four Bar-D riders showed up in the middle of the afternoon. Ed Gilman was one of them.

Pete frowned to the kid, barefoot in his long underwear, sitting on a length of log next to the fire. "Wait right there." Pete stood up and walked out to meet the riders.

The man who had done the talking in town spurred his horse forward and stopped in front of Pete. "Looks like you're harborin' a criminal here."

"Is that right?"

"Yes, it is."

"What crime?"

"We found this kid and another one puttin' a rope on a calf this mornin'. Chased 'em to the river. The other kid went under, him and his horse. They fished 'em out down river a couple of miles. This one got past us."

"So what do you want now?"

The rider swung down from his horse. He was not a big man, but he had the lean, hard build of a man who spent long hours on horseback. "I want to talk to this kid," he said as he pulled at the cuffs of his leather gloves.

The other three men had come to a stop and dismounted. One of them took the reins from the lead man.

Pete swept over the four of them, meeting eyes with Ed Gilman and then coming back to the leader. "Just remember, you're not the law," he said. Then he stepped to the side and turned to the kid. "This man wants to talk to you."

The kid sat with his hands on his knees for a few seconds, as if he didn't want to leave the fire, and then he pushed himself up onto his feet. He took short, uncertain steps across the wood chips and twigs until he stood in the dirt in front of the Bar-D rider.

"Are you the one that ran from us this morning? You and your friend?"

The kid looked at the ground. "I guess so."

"Look up at me!"

The kid raised his head.

"Your friend's dead. You know that?"

"Yeh."

"What?"

"Yes, sir."

The rider held his head up and looked down his nose. "Tryin' to make easy money. Were you doin' it for someone else, or just yourselves?"

"Just ourselves."

"You have your own brand, then?" The man sniffed, short.

"We had one we could use."

"What brand was it?"

"I'm not sure. Jesse knew it and how to make it."

"Where's the runnin' iron?"

"Jesse had it."

"We didn't find it on him or the horse either one."

"Well, he had it. You can search my things."

"And I suppose it was his rope, too."

"Yes, sir. I still have mine."

"You're just a snivelin' little son of a bitch, aren't you? Blame it all on your buddy, when he's dead and gone."

"He was my—"

The man's fist came out of nowhere and caught the kid on the jaw, spinning him halfway around and backward. The man moved to his saddle, took down his coiled rope, and walked over to where the boy was coming up on all fours. Using the rope, the Bar-D rider slapped him with a fierce blow on the face, neck, and shoulder, and the kid went down. The man stood over him and slapped him again, again, and again. Each time, the kid yelped, and after the last swat he lay sobbing with his face in the dirt.

The man held back the rope as if he was ready to swing again as soon as the kid moved.

"I think that's gone far enough," said Pete.

The man with the rope turned and gave a hard stare. "You stay out of this, you hear?"

"Like I said before, you're not the law. Maybe this kid laid a hand, or tried to lay a hand, on your boss's property, but this is my land, and I'm not going to stand by and let someone take things too far."

The Bar-D man's neck and ears had turned red. "So you think you can tell me how far to take things?"

"Look. The one kid died, and you've beat this one into the ground. What more do you want?"

The man raised his coiled rope to waist level and shook it. "I want to teach this kid a lesson early on, so it'll do him some good."

Pete looked down at the kid. "I'd say you've already done it."

Ed Gilman spoke up. "I'd say that's right, Van. I think the rest of us have seen enough, too."

The man named Van looked around at his fellow riders. Then with his gloved fist he shook the rope above the kid's face. "I hope you've learned something." He took the reins from the other rider and snapped up onto his saddle. With a final glare at Pete, he spun his horse away and took off at a lope.

The kid was still shaking when Pete got him seated on the log again.

"All the time—he was whipping me—all I could think of—was how I was cheating—and Jesse was dead—and I was getting whipped—like a baby."

"You can't help what happened to your partner. He got it worse than you did, but you took your licks too. That's what you've got to do."

"He just whipped me—like a little kid. I'm no good."

"Well, stealin' cattle's no good, but you can be done with that if you want to. Just pull yourself together."

"I'm no good."

"It's prob'ly natural that you feel that way right now. You need to let a little water seep back into the well."

"Tell me about water." And he started sobbing again.

"Look, kid, I'm sorry for your partner. But you've got your own self to look out for, try to get straight."

The kid shook his head and moaned.

"This might be the lowest day you'll ever know, but even if it isn't, you've got to build up from here."

The kid sniffed, cleared his throat, and spit off to the side. His voice was steady as he said, "I'm nothin'. I've got nothin'. Never did. There's nothin' to build on."

"Then you've got to dig deep. You can't do it all at once. You can stay here as long as you want. Let it all settle in."

"That's the last thing I'd want to do. Stay around here."

"Look at me, kid. Look me in the eye."

The kid turned his miserable gaze toward Pete, who stood to one side of the fire. The light of the flames, even in daylight, played a ghostly flicker on the kid's features.

"You've got to look life in the face, just like you're lookin' at me, just like you had to look at that man who whipped you."

"You talk like you know everything."

"I don't. But I know a couple of things." Pete paused for a breath and went on. "I was in trouble once, too, and after I took my medicine I tried to leave the whole thing behind. I came here. I met a girl. I thought she cared for me, and she probably did. Then another fella found out about my past and gloated about it to me, in front of her. She dropped me, went with him." He took a breath and went on. "I lost my sense of worth, let the man push me around, and when the shame got too much for me to stand, I went away. But I didn't do any good nursing my sorrows. What I had to do was look into myself and decide what I was worth. After that I could hold my head up."

"What was wrong with the first time you took off, when you wanted to put it behind you?"

"Nothin' at the time, except it helped me think I could run from my troubles. That was my mistake when I tried it again."

"So you came back, to a place that doesn't even have water."

"I came back to face up to myself, back to the place where I ran from my shame. As for this place, there's nothing wrong with it, as long as a fella doesn't mind haulin' his own water for a while." Pete saw the kid's face go pale again. "What's the matter?"

"I just can't get it out of my mind, what happened to Jesse."

Pete recalled the sentence that got cut short. "Was he your brother?"

"No, he wasn't. But he was all I had. Now I've got nothin'. Nowhere to go, and this is the last place in the world I'd want to stay."

"Sleep on it, then. Give yourself a day or two, anyway. Don't be in a hurry to run if you've got nowhere to run to. I can understand you wantin' to put this town behind you, but don't make runnin' a way of life. How old are you, anyway?"

"Seventeen."

"About what I thought. Hate to see you turn into a saddle tramp so young."

The kid shivered and leaned toward the fire. "And what about you?"

"I'm almost twice that age."

"No, I mean, you say you faced up to it. But what are you goin' to do on a place like this?"

"Oh, I'll find work. Sooner or later I'll put in a windmill, learn how that works. Sometimes I wish the stream would come back this way again, but I'm sure not goin' to wait for it. There's more than one way to get your water."

Emma's Purpose

For most of the time that my sister and I were growing up in Cold Springs, it was an uneventful place. The freight wagons rolled in and rolled out, and the stagecoach made its stops, but not much changed. Sometimes we would see a new face in town, and then after a week or a month or three months, the person would be gone and the town would go on like before. The woman named Emma seemed, at first, like one more in a long series of strangers who came and went. She must have come in on the stagecoach, because one Sunday when Rebecca and I went to the Owl Café, Emma served us our fried chicken and hot biscuits.

We saw her there again the next Sunday, and the Sunday after that. She seemed like a patient woman, always willing to stand by and listen to whatever we might have to say. We explained that we came to eat on Sundays because it was Edith's day off and she went out to the country to spend the day with her family. We also mentioned that it was the day when our father had dinner with some of the other men, in something like a club.

We didn't explain that they liked to keep to themselves, out of the public eye, where they could eat good steak, drink wine and brandy, and speak among themselves. I guess we figured Emma could figure that out for herself, just as she could find out, from a bit of gossip here and there, that the other men in the group did not feel an urgent need to spend

Sunday at home. A couple of them, ranch men, did not have wives; one of them, the judge, had a nervous wife who kept the house closed up; and one of them, a storekeeper, had a wife who was rumored to drink early on Sundays. They were all men—including our father—who took some trouble to keep up a good appearance, and one way to do that was to have a version of a gentlemen's club in Cold Springs. We assumed, I guess, that if Emma stayed in town very long she would find out well enough who was who.

We told her other things, such as how our mother had died when we were young, back in Illinois, and how our father had taken us out west when he had this good opportunity. Drayage, we explained to her, was the word for the freight business, and Charles Addison was our father. She could see the sign for Addison Drayage from inside the café. She said it must have been hard to grow up in a frontier town without a mother, and we said we guessed we were used to it, that our father made sure we were well provided for. We didn't tell her how it was quite a point with him that he had raised us himself—with the help of Edith and other rawboned working girls before her—and that he hadn't left us with relatives or at an orphanage, although, as he reminded us from time to time, he could have. It smarted when he said those things, and they weren't the kinds of comments a young person would want to repeat to a stranger. And even though Emma seemed interested in whatever we had to say, she seemed to sense the things that we would just as soon leave alone.

If someone had asked me, after those first three Sundays, what sort of a person Emma was, I would have said she was a nice woman—I don't know if I would have said a lady, as she worked in a café—and I might have described her as the kind of person who would be the mother of a friend. She was kind and concerned and never went too far, and all in all she seemed like quite an improvement over the common kind of biscuit-shooter that came and went in places like the Owl Café.

If someone had asked me if I liked her, the question would have made me uncomfortable, for the truth was that I liked her quite a bit, in a secret way. I liked her dark hairline and her blue eyes, the texture of her skin, the slope of her neck. She had good posture and a high, pert bosom that my eyes came back to, time and again. But then her eyes always met mine, and she would smile as if to say it was all right, she understood, and we could go on with whatever we were talking about.

By the time Rebecca and I had been to the Owl Café three times, I had begun to feel a very strong pull toward this woman. In the year or so before that, I had been with a couple of women—the kind that work in road ranches—so I knew a little of what was possible. But I had also been in the presence of women who had a great deal more mystery and power than the common janes, and this woman Emma was one of those who, as I sensed it, could unveil some of the richest secrets. There were nights when I could not go to sleep well into the wee hours, tossing and thinking, imagining how I would be enveloped in wonder if she would take me to her magic.

This urge grew so strong in me that I took it upon myself to walk by the café, front and back, at various hours, to see if

I could get a chance at seeing her when she was not engaged by work. After a couple of days of restless walks and nervous glances, I saw her one afternoon. She was sitting on an up-turned crate in back of the café, taking in the sun and smoking a tailor-made cigarette.

We waved to each other, and I walked over to talk to her. She squinted a little as she looked up at me with the sun in her face, but she was smiling in the way she had of making me feel comfortable. She asked what I was doing, and I said I was out on a walk, trying to clear the cobwebs. She said she was doing the same thing. I noticed her hands, rough and reddened from her work, but they did not make her any less appealing. She was a full-bodied woman, and as far as I knew, she was free to receive attention.

I went on to ask her if she didn't get lonely in this town, and she said, yes, sometimes. She said she imagined I had plenty of friends and no worries about how to fill the time. I agreed, but I added that there always seemed to be something missing. She didn't answer, just took a puff on her cigarette, and I felt a bold surge flow through me.

"Don't you ever feel that way?" I asked.

"What way?"

"That you wished you had company."

She shrugged.

"I mean, sometimes I wish I could meet someone—no, I mean, meet *with* someone, a person I knew, just to be with. Oh, I don't think I'm making sense."

She gave me a smile, but not an inviting one. "I think I know what you mean, Eddie."

This was my only chance, I thought. If this moment passed, there might not be another. I heard myself saying, "Just to meet, and be together, with no one else around. Away from everything."

She nodded, but it didn't mean what I wished it did.

"Don't you ever feel that way?" I asked.

"Oh, I don't know. Not now—or not lately, anyway."

I held my hand out toward her, and she put the tips of the fingers of her reddened left hand against mine. In spite of the texture, her hand looked slender and graceful.

As her eyes met mine, I asked, "Not even once?"

She smiled and gave a light shake to her head as she took her hand away. "You're going to do fine, Eddie. You can have your pick of women. You can have any one you want."

I tried to hold her with my eyes as I said, "But you don't know what I want."

"Oh, yes, I do," she answered, with the kind of tone that said everything was all right, in spite of my awkwardness. "It just wouldn't be a good thing for either of us to have done. But it makes for a nice thought."

"I must seem like a kid to you."

"Not in every way, and to tell you the truth, I find it flattering."

"But it's still just a nice thought."

"Yes, but it's a nice one. Not the other kind."

I didn't go looking for her after that, and I was afraid of how I would act if I met her unexpectedly on the street. I knew that if she was still at the café the next Sunday she would put me at ease in front of my sister, so I didn't dread seeing

113

her. I was just afraid to see her by accident because I felt so green and clumsy.

I was in for a big surprise, then, when a couple of days later she showed up at our house. When I opened the front door I didn't recognize her at first, as she was dressed better than at work. She was wearing what I would think of as traveling clothes—a broadcloth jacket and long skirt, and a drab-colored blouse that did not damage her appearance. She was carrying a handbag, and I suppose that gave her the appearance of a traveler as well, or even more so the look of a woman from beyond the world of Cold Springs and the Owl Café. All in an instant as I recognized her I saw the dark brown hair, the blue eyes, and the clear, open expression of her face. My heart was beating fast, but I was not afraid, because her smile told me not to be.

As I smiled back at her, I caught a movement to the side and in back of her. There stood a serious-looking man, tall and heavy-browed, wearing a business suit and holding a small valise, the likes of which land agents and lawyers carried around.

"Good afternoon, Eddie," she said. "This is Mr. Liggett. I was wondering if we could come in and talk for a few minutes." Then, as she must have noticed my expression change, she added, "It's not about anything you and I have talked about."

"Oh." I nodded and stepped aside, and as I did so I wondered if I should have. My father was not home yet, and I did not know if he knew these people. But they were coming inside.

Rebecca's voice came from the top of the stairs. "Who's there, Eddie?"

"It's Emma," I called back.

"Oh." Then my sister came into view, taking light, quick steps down the staircase.

Emma and Mr. Liggett each took a straight-backed chair, and Rebecca and I sat on the sofa.

"Is your father at home?" asked Emma.

"No," I answered. "But I expect him pretty soon."

She looked around the room. "Well, it's with him that we want to talk."

I nodded as I reviewed what she had just said about there not being anything about the visit I had with her. Taking things at their face value, I decided that she had something unrelated to discuss with our father and would bide her time with us in the meanwhile. While my sister and I were old enough to be considered young adults, we were still being left to sit on the sofa and engage in small talk while this older person waited to state her business with our father. It made me feel something like a kid, being deferred like that, but at the same time the presence of the woman left me feeling nervous.

"Let me see what Edith's got," I said, getting up and heading for the kitchen.

Mr. Liggett tipped me a nod, and Emma turned her smile from me to my sister.

I found Edith and asked her to set out some tea things, and then I went back to the sitting room. At that moment, my father came in through the front door, and the silence hung in the room as he took off his hat and looked at the visitors.

"Are you Charles Addison?" asked Mr. Liggett, rising.

"Yes, I am."

"I'm Robert Liggett, attorney-at-law, and I represent this person here, whom I think you know."

To my surprise, my father gave Emma a brief glance and then nodded to her lawyer.

"Well, then, if you don't mind, we can sit down and get things under way."

"I don't know what there is to talk about," said my father, giving a narrow look, "or whether Rebecca and Eddie need to be part of it."

Emma raised her eyebrows and said, "Oh, they've already been brought into it."

My heart gave a lurch, but I held my jaws tight. I didn't know what Emma meant, but looking back on it, I think she just wanted to keep us in the room.

My father's eyes darted at each of us. "What have you heard?"

"Nothing," I said.

Rebecca shook her head and repeated, "Nothing."

I crossed the rug and sat down by my sister again, while my father, who seemed to have been caught off guard, gave another sharp look at Emma and Mr. Liggett.

"I don't know what purpose you intend to serve, or why you assume I can be expected to sit through it," he said.

Mr. Liggett lifted his chin. "I think you have a pretty good idea of why you can be expected to give her an audience."

"Oh, I do?"

"I don't think you are prepared to deny that you and she are still married, under the law of the state of Illinois."

My father's face had gone hard as a stone, and he did not speak. I looked at Emma, wondering what it meant for me, but I could read nothing at that moment. I felt my head begin to swim.

"And that one of these children is the issue of that marriage."

My sister and I looked at each other, and I felt a prickly fear crawl through me. I dared not look at Emma then.

"You can't come into my house and make me admit whatever claims you throw out."

"Well, then, we'll go at it a step at a time."

"What for? As far as we've been concerned, she's been dead." My father gave a look of contempt. "Anyone who has spent sixteen years in prison can't expect any more than that."

"Very well. One step at a time. Or if you wish, we can bring it up in front of a judge. I understand you know one."

My father glared at Emma. "What do you want?"

She maintained a calm front as she let her lawyer speak.

"What my client wants is to make herself known to her child."

"To what purpose?"

"That *is* the purpose."

"And a very poor one."

"Be that as it may, we hope to proceed. You cannot deny, then, that you were, have been, and still are married to this woman?"

"Why should I?"

Now I dared to look at Emma, and she gave me an expression that said, "Don't worry."

"Nor can you deny that, some sixteen years ago and more, there was another woman, what some people would call a mistress—"

"She was not my mistress."

"Or a lover."

"She was not my lover."

"Nevertheless, there was another woman, and you knew her quite well."

"She was not what you say."

"Quite well enough, in fact, to have a child with her."

"You can't prove any of that."

I could feel my sister trembling as she took my hand. I had gotten my own head to stop swimming, but I imagined she was still dizzied by the rush of statements.

Mr. Liggett opened his valise. "Certificates of birth from the state of Illinois, Mr. Addison. You had a child with this other woman, your mistress."

"She was not my mistress."

"Well, then, we shall just call her the other woman."

"She can't speak for herself." My father's eyes burned a beam of hatred at Emma. "*She* made sure of that."

"No, she can't. She's been dead these sixteen years, and as the surviving parent, you had a right to take the child. My client has no quarrel with that."

"Well, how considerate." Then, with a sneer, "They should have kept her locked up."

"My client has paid her debt."

"Oh, has she? And what is the debt? How much? What price do you put on it?"

"It was a fair trial, as you yourself know, having testified in it."

I had the feeling that Mr. Liggett was saying more than he needed to, for the benefit of Rebecca and me.

"Fair indeed. And now she's free, even though she killed a woman." My father raised his chin and gave a look of reproach.

"The jury made its decision, and my client has paid her debt."

My father's expression clouded, and his eyes narrowed. "The jury decided it was not premeditated, but she had to have stalked Louisa to know which train she was taking, and then to board the train, and wait until it reached full speed, and then to wrestle her out onto the landing—oh, come on, now, if it wasn't an act of premeditated violence."

I had the feeling now that my father was the one who wanted to say things for the benefit of the audience.

Mr. Liggett went on, unruffled. "She had her motives, but the altercation itself was spontaneous. That has all been settled in court. But I cannot blame you for your bitterness, for you must have cared for the woman who, had it not been for your illicit love—"

"She was not my lover!"

"Then how came it to be that you had a child with her?"

My father sat stone-faced as before, clenching his teeth.

"A baby boy. Not a year older, in fact, than his sister, whom you had with this woman who now sits here in our presence."

I looked at Rebecca, who was shaking her head. I could tell she was drifting and had not yet taken in the full meaning. We had been raised with the knowledge that our mother, something of a sainted figure, had died when we were young. Now, in a few minutes, what we thought we knew had been shaken to its roots, and the shaking was deeper for my sister than for me.

Rebecca's face was clouded as she spoke to me. "I don't—I just don't—"

"He had two women," I said.

"Two wives?"

I looked at my father and back at my sister. "No. One wife, and another woman."

She put her hand to her mouth. "Then we're not—"

"Yes, we are. We still are. But not exactly the same way we thought."

Mr. Liggett cut in. "Rebecca, this is your mother."

A wave of agony crossed my sister's face as she looked at Emma. I could tell that in that moment she recognized not only the truth of who her mother was but also the truth of who she herself was.

"You," she said. "You are my mother."

Emma gave a solemn nod.

"My mother is a —"

"A murderess," said my father. "That's what she is. A convict. A criminal."

Rebecca wore an expression of pain and disgust. "And you came here, all smiles, to make friends with us, and all the time you were just spying."

"I had to look things over first. I don't expect you to like any part of this, but I felt I had to do it."

"Why?"

"Just so you would know that your mother—what little she has been your actual mother—is not dead. I just thought you should have that knowledge."

Rebecca's face was clouded. "What good does it do?" she asked.

"Maybe none."

My father cut in. "You've got a lot of cheek, Emma, deciding what she does and doesn't need to know."

Emma had a calm demeanor as she looked straight at my father. "It's nothing but the truth, and that's something you've never liked very much."

My father turned toward Mr. Liggett. "Well, have you achieved your purpose? Made this girl's life miserable, and shamed me in front of my children?"

"As my client said, her purpose was to bring out the truth. And to let things fall as they may."

Emma looked at Rebecca. "Like I said, I don't expect you to like me or anything I've done. But I'll be at the hotel for two days more, in case you'd like to say something or send a message. If you don't, I'll understand. And I won't trouble you any more." She stood up and held her hand out. "Goodbye."

My sister just sat where she was, with tears falling from her eyes as she shook her head.

Emma turned to me. "Good-bye, Eddie. I'm sorry for any pain I've caused you."

I shrugged. "I don't know yet."

Mr. Liggett was standing now, looming over us with his heavy brows. "My office is in Omaha," he said, taking me in with the others. Then he ushered Emma out the front door.

I did not see her again. I suppose she stayed the two days, and then she was gone for sure. I could feel it. But things did not go back to being the way they had been, to say the least.

It was much harder for my sister than it was for me. For my part, it was mainly a matter of adjusting what I thought I knew about other people. My father was a cad and a liar, my mother was not quite the saint I had thought, and Emma was not just a person who had come to town to work in the Owl Café. But my mother was indeed dead, although under worse circumstances than I had been led to believe, and my sister was still my sister.

Rebecca, on the other hand, had to accept the truth that this woman, revealed as a murderess and a convict, was of her blood. That was the hardest, and she told me more than once that Emma was coarse and her mother in name only. As for herself, she said she was going to be a good woman, no thanks to either parent. Within a year she had married a young surveyor and had gone off to Colorado, and now I hear from her about once a year.

I stayed on a little longer than she did, working in my father's office as before. I cannot say I ever understood him;

that is, I could never understand how he could believe that he could leave the truth behind and then deny it when it caught up with him. He should have known it would all come around, that matters so deep and serious were bound to follow him.

I believe also that he should have known better than to think he could justify all the lies by saying, as he did, that he kept up the pretense because he loved his children. I think he had himself convinced that he was doing it to protect us and that doing it in the name of family made everything all right.

As for Emma, I have often wondered about her purpose and thought about how she held to it. I do not doubt that her main motive was, as she said, to make herself known to her child and to bring out the truth, even though her doing so wrecked any chance at reclaiming her daughter. Nor could I overlook that she was a vengeful woman and that she must have taken some satisfaction in ruining my father's false respectability. But I respect her for not doing what she could have done to spite Louisa and Charles that day when she was smoking a tailor-made cigarette and had it all at her fingertips.

Not Going Anywhere

Blaine led the old sorrel horse into the corral, turned it, and slipped off the halter. He stepped backward and closed the gate. As he turned away from sliding the latch, a speck in the distance caught his eye. He watched it as he walked to the cabin. Once inside, he hung the halter and rope on a nail, glanced to see that the Spencer .38 was resting on its pegs, and took his place by the window.

The speck had grown larger, and he could see that it consisted of two riders coming his way across the dry plains from the east. He waited, drumming his fingers on the window frame. The horses were not moving very fast.

He turned away to see if anything in the room needed attention in case he invited the travelers in. When he looked out again, the riders were gone. Then they came up out of a dip in the ground. The horse on the left was a bay, reddish-brown with a black mane and tail. The other was a brown with a white blaze on its forehead and socks in front. The man on the right was bigger than the one on the left.

Closer now, a quarter of a mile away, the man on the right had a familiar shape and posture. It looked like Tom. The man's hat brim lifted, and Blaine was sure it was his brother. Three years were gone like that, and here was Tom riding up to his front door.

Blaine stepped outside to meet his visitors. The horses plodded forward. Tom raised his hand in greeting, and Blaine waved. When the horses came to a stop and the riders swung down, Blaine saw that Tom's partner was a little fellow, short and slender and hawkish.

Tom called out in a cheerful tone. "Billy! What the hell!"

"Hey, Tom." Blaine reached out and shook his brother's hand.

"This is my pal Chip," Tom said as he turned. "Chip, this is my brother Billy."

Blaine held out his hand. "Blaine Duchamp. Tom calls me Billy."

"Pleased to meet you." Chip held out his gloved hand, and his eyes drifted over Blaine. "I can see the family resemblance," he said. "Tom says nothing but good things about you."

"Well, let's put your horses up. I'm sure they can use a drink."

"That's right," said Tom. "Long, hot ride."

"Where you comin' from?"

"Nebraska. Just as well been New Mexico. Country's burnin' up."

Blaine took a quick glance. Tom's face had gotten plenty of sun, and it seemed fuller than the last time Blaine had seen him.

"Well, no worry. There's water enough for you and your horses."

"That's what I told Chip. I said, 'You can have a whole gallon to wash your face.'"

"That's right." Blaine smiled. "Let's take the horses this way."

* * * * *

During supper, as the three men went at the fried beef and potatoes, Blaine asked how long the travelers meant to stay.

Tom frowned. "Not long. Prob'ly just tonight."

"Oh. Are you pressed for time?"

Chip didn't look up.

Tom said, "Kind of."

"Why don't you stay over a day, let your horses rest up?"

"We'd like to, but we've got jobs waitin' for us. If we don't get there on time, he might hire someone else."

Chip still didn't look up.

Tom put on a smile. "This is sure good grub, Billy."

"Yeah, it is," Chip added.

"Glad you like it. If I'd known you were coming, I might have made a pie."

"Next time." Tom picked at his teeth with his knife. "Probably come back here in the fall, stay a few days. Huh, Chip."

"Oh, yeah."

* * * * *

The first light of dawn was showing in the window when Blaine poured the coffee. "Hot biscuits comin' up," he said.

Tom showed his broad smile. "Just the way we like 'em."

Chip came back from the doorway where he had been smoking a cigarette. He sniffed and sat down.

Blaine set the coffee pot on top of the stove, then opened the oven and took out two tin plates with half a dozen biscuits on each.

"Get started on these," he said. "I'll put in another dozen, and you'll have some for the trail."

"Ah, Billy, you don't have to go to that much trouble."

Blaine set a crockery jar on the table. "Here's some rhubarb jam. Gal that makes it could learn to cook the rhubarb a little longer, but it's all right."

"Gal of yours?"

"No, just a gal who does cookin' and sewin' and tries to make a livin'."

"I'm sure it'll taste good."

When Blaine took his seat at the table, a third of the biscuits were gone but the jam jar had gone down very little. He took a biscuit for himself and smeared some jam on top. He was biting the chunk of rhubarb in two when Tom spoke.

"I was wonderin', Billy, what you'd think of tradin' horses."

Blaine chewed the rhubarb and got it down. "You mean my two for your two?"

"Yeah. We've still got a ways to go, and fresh horses would help."

Blaine took a drink of coffee. "I don't know. I think your two horses are better than mine, or they will be when they get rested up. That sorrel of mine is gettin' pretty old, and I don't know if he'll tire out on you. The buckskin, he's all right, just don't give him any play."

127

Tom reached for another biscuit. "Chip can ride the sorrel. He's light in the ass, and that horse won't know he's got a load on him. Huh, Chip?"

"Sure."

"Nothing wrong with these two you've been riding?"

"Oh, no," said Tom. "We come a long way on 'em, and no trouble." He bit into his biscuit.

"I mean—"

"Oh. Nah, neither of 'em has got a brand on 'im, so we didn't even bother with papers. But I'll give you a bill of sale if you want."

"Where do they come from?"

"Wichita."

"Oh, I see. You went up to Nebraska and then came here?"

"That's right. But these horses are clean as can be."

Blaine looked from Tom to Chip and then back to Tom. "Oh, I guess so."

"Thanks," said Tom. He finished his biscuit and dusted his fingers. "It'll be a great help. And we can trade back in the fall if you're not pleased."

* * * * *

The sun had cleared the hills in the east when Tom and Chip led their horses away from the hitching rail.

Tom held out his hand to shake his brother's. "Thanks for everything, Billy. We'll see you on the way back through.

Stay a few days, help you out with anything that needs to be done."

"Sure." Blaine released his handshake and turned to Chip. "Good luck to you, and I hope that horse works out for you. He hangs his head, but if you keep at him he'll lift it up and move along."

"I'm sure he'll be fine. I'm easy on a horse." Chip took a final drag on his cigarette, tossed the snipe on the ground, and stepped on it. He held out his hand. "Thanks for everything, and we'll see you next time." As soon as he finished shaking, he stepped back and put on his gloves.

The two travelers mounted up, waved, and took off at a trot toward the Dettman Buttes. Blaine watched them until they disappeared behind a rise. That was the way Tom was. Ever since he was old enough to leave home, he was in a hurry to be gone, and most of the time he was running from trouble. Like the old saying went, he was getting nowhere fast.

* * * * *

Blaine was not surprised the next day when he saw a lone rider coming from the east. The man was on a big horse the color of dark honey, and he was moving at a brisk walk.

At fifty yards out, the rider drew rein and called a greeting.

Blaine stepped outside and waved him into the yard.

The horse walked the rest of the way until the man said, "Whoa." The horse stopped, and the man swung down.

He was a slender man, about average height. He wore a dark, round-brimmed hat with a peaked crown. When he tipped his hat back, the sunlight fell on his features. He had large eyes, prominent cheekbones, an aquiline nose, and a bushy mustache that spilled over and around his mouth. He wore a grey cotton shirt with a stub collar, plus a brown leather vest that matched his belt and holster.

He waved the tips of his reins and said, "Afternoon."

"Good afternoon."

"Name's Potter."

Blaine tipped his head in acknowledgment. "Blaine Duchamp. What can I do for you?"

"Lookin' for a couple of fellas that might have come this way. My guess would be day before yesterday."

"What do they look like?"

"One of 'em, about your description—height, weight, and dark hair. The other's a little fella, brown-haired and hatchet-faced."

"Are you a lawman?"

"Not exactly. But I work on the side of the law. I bring in men that are wanted."

"When there's a reward."

Potter twisted his mouth, and the mustache moved. "Can't afford to do it for free. My percentage rate's low enough as it is."

"I imagine."

"So I was wonderin' if you seen anyone like these two fellas."

"What are their names?"

"The little one is Fenwick, and the other is Burns."

Blaine didn't see any point in lying to a man who was a tracker. "I'll tell you, a couple of riders did come by, but they didn't mention any last names."

"Fenwick goes by Chip. His pals with a great sense of humor call him Splinter. The other one's Tom."

"That might be them."

"Ridin' a bay horse and a brown."

Blaine was glad he hadn't started out lying. "They were. In fact, they traded with me. I've got those two horses in my corral."

"What did they leave on?"

"A buckskin and a sorrel."

Potter's eyebrows lifted. "Which way did they go?"

"They said they were going to go out through the buttes."

"Men like them don't usually go the way they say. That's rough country, isn't it?"

"I believe so."

Potter looked up at the sun. "Well, I think I'd better move on. I'd appreciate it if I could water my horse."

"You're welcome to stay."

"Thanks, but I'm used to sleepin' on the ground. Hear better that way, 'specially if someone's comin'."

"I'll show you to the water."

As the yellowish-brown horse drank from the trough, Potter looked over the two horses in the corral. Then his gaze wandered out to the buttes and back.

"That's enough," he said. He tugged on the reins, and his horse's muzzle came up dripping. As he led the horse aside, he glanced at Blaine and said, "You don't ask many questions."

"Doesn't pay well enough."

Potter laughed. "That doesn't stop most people." He turned to the horse and tightened the cinch, then put his foot in the stirrup. "Well, thanks, friend. And so long."

"Good luck. If you come back this way, drop in."

* * * * *

When Blaine went out to do the chores the next morning, the old sorrel horse was standing by the corral. It gave him pause. The horse did not have a saddle, bridle, or neck rope on him. Blaine figured the animal had been turned loose, and Fenwick, if he was still riding, was mounted on something better—either a buckskin or a tall horse the color of dark honey.

Blaine gave the sorrel a good looking-over and found no telltale marks. The horse might have a story to tell if he could talk, but to all appearances, he had just come home. Blaine put him in the corral, gave grain to all three horses, and pumped water into the trough.

Back in the cabin, he fidgeted as he waited for the coffee to brew. He broke a cold biscuit and ate it, then another. The coffee boiled, and he sprinkled cold water on top. He told himself not to hurry, but he burned his tongue on the coffee anyway. He set the cup aside and laid out a cotton sack on his bed. He put in a shirt, a wool overshirt, and a pair of socks, then rolled up the sack. He folded a pair of blankets length-wise and rolled them up. Then he drank the coffee and took the .38 Spencer from its pegs.

He rode the brown horse his brother had left behind. The trail through the Dettman Buttes took him into rough country, as Potter had said. The grass was sparse, and the prickly pear cactus grew close to the ground. The grey dust rose in thin, powdery wisps. The brown horse had rested up, but by mid-morning he had worked up quite a sweat and was breathing hard. Blaine knew of a place where in good years water stayed in a pool late in the summer.

He kept the horse going for two more hours until he reached the spot. It was a grassy area about a hundred yards wide, surrounded by sandstone. A dozen crevices led into it, but only one trail went in and out. Along the west side, box elder trees and chokecherry bushes grew in a gravel wash. Blaine found the pool, shallow and tepid, and let the horse drink.

On the other side of the pool, a sandstone wall rose straight up and reflected the mid-day heat. Blaine moved to-ward a lower formation of rocks on the west side where he thought he might sit in the shade.

The brown horse whickered, and Blaine saw motion in a shadowy cleft to his right.

"So you decided to come after all," said a droll voice. A man stepped forward, and Blaine recognized the dark peaked hat and the bushy mustache. Potter moved out from a screen of chokecherry bushes, and his honey-colored horse followed.

"The sorrel horse I traded came back to my place," said Blaine. "I back-tracked him to here."

"Ain't it funny. They went the way they said. But the trail thins out from here. Can't find any tracks leadin' out. It's as if he rode right up over the rocks."

"He?"

"Oh, yeah. Only one man rode out of here. Like you said, the other horse went back your way." Potter poked his cheek out with his tongue.

"He's an old horse. The buckskin's quite a bit better for this kind of travel, I'd think." Blaine's eyes rested on Potter. "If only one man left, where's the other?"

"Over yonder. Under a pile of rocks."

Blaine flinched, and he followed the motion of Potter's head. "Which one of 'em is it?"

Potter shrugged. "Don't know. If it was a colder time of year, I might want to take a look. But he's not goin' anywhere, and I can pick him up later. I need another horse for that, anyway."

"Well, what do you plan to do, then?"

"Go after the fella on the buckskin horse."

"But if you don't know where he's going?"

"Oh, I never said that."

"So you do know?"

"I've got a hunch."

"Where's that?"

"Claybank."

"Why would they go there?"

"See? You *are* like everyone else."

"What do you mean by that?"

"You ask a lot of questions."

"Well, it seems as if there's a lot to be asked."

"I suppose there are." Potter drew out a curved-stem pipe and an oilskin tobacco pouch. "But I don't mind lettin' someone else ask 'em. Let's go over here and sit in the shade." Potter led the way to the other side of the open spot where an upthrust of rock cast a narrow shadow.

When they sat down, Blaine spoke first. "Why would these two be going to Claybank?"

"What did they did tell you?"

"They said they had a job waiting, but they didn't say where."

"Pah! Some job. They had an old crony they wanted to catch up with."

"Really?"

"Yep. Here's the deal." Potter stuffed tobacco into the bowl of his pipe. "I'll tell it straight out rather than make you ask questions all day, though it's a fun game." He struck a match and drew a thick puff of smoke. "Your acquaintances Burns and Fenwick were spending some time in Kansas, but they got out before they were supposed to."

"What were they in for?"

"A little hold-up job. They made two mistakes. One, they shot a teller. Two, they had a partner who was willin' to squeal on 'em. He made a deal and high-tailed it, and when they broke out, they headed this way."

"And the squealer, he lives in Claybank?"

"That's my information."

"What's his name?"

"Ed Timothy."

Blaine shook his head. "Never heard of him."

"Neither had I. And I've never seen any of 'em. Just posters of Burns and Fenwick. I've got 'em along if you want to see 'em."

"Nah. I know what they look like." Blaine glanced toward the pile of rocks. "I sure wonder which one has gone under, though."

"You can go look. All the same to me."

"No. I'll wait."

"I can't guarantee I'll go back your way when I'm done."

"No, I mean I'll wait till we get to Claybank."

"Oh, so you want to ride on, uh?"

"I want to see who's riding that buckskin." Blaine hoped it was Tom, but he feared it wasn't. If Tom was over there underneath a pile of rocks, Blaine didn't want to see him—not in the presence of a bounty hunter. And if Tom was the one who rode out of here, Blaine might be able to help him keep from getting hurt.

* * * * *

Blaine and Potter rode on through the Dettman Buttes and came out on the west side in early evening. They camped on Dettman Creek, where they picketed the horses and got a small campfire going. Blaine ate cold biscuits, and Potter ate some hard crusts of bread.

In the course of conversation, Blaine said, "Just on the face of it, I would never have guessed those two fellows did what you said they did."

"Probably at one time, they would never have guessed they'd end up like that some day. But once they did, they had time to think about it. They were in the hoosegow for damn near a year, and it didn't make 'em any better."

"It's too bad they go that way. You figure every one of 'em is someone's son, and most of 'em are someone's brother."

"Yeah," said Potter, "but they make their choices. And most of 'em couldn't care less about the heartache they cause. It's a lucky family member who never has to know."

"I suppose," said Blaine. "But the ones who don't know always wonder. At least the ones who do know don't have any illusions."

"If it was me—ah, hell, what's the use? It isn't."

* * * * *

They headed north the next day and rode into Claybank in the middle of the afternoon. Potter was swaying in the saddle in his easy-going way.

"I think the first thing to do," he said, drawing his words out, "is to find somethin' to eat. Then ask around for this fella Ed Timothy."

Blaine stopped his horse.

Potter drew rein and turned his head. "What is it?"

137

Blaine nodded toward the hitch rack ahead on their left. In a low voice he said, "That's the buckskin I traded to those two."

"Well, now." Potter leaned forward, grabbed the saddle horn with both hands, and swung down, all slow and careful.

Blaine stepped down as well, then crossed in front of his horse to stand next to Potter. Straight in front of the buckskin was the dark doorway of a saloon. Blaine spoke in an even lower voice than before. "Shall we both go in?"

Potter spoke out of the side of his mouth. "I think it'd be better if you waited out here."

"I'd like to go in. In case it's Burns."

Potter took in a breath through his nose as he turned his head. His large eyes met Blaine's. "He's your brother, isn't he? Well, don't worry. I won't shoot him. I'll tell him you're waitin' out here." Potter's eyes flickered toward the saloon and back. "But if it's not him, it's just as well you don't get in the way."

"How about if I just go up and look through the door?"

Potter shook his head. "No, Fenwick knows you. If he sees you, things get a lot harder. Better you stay here. I've done this before, so let me do it." He handed the reins to Blaine and walked away. He stepped up onto the board side-walk, brushed his hand across the handle of his six-gun, and pushed open the swinging doors of the saloon.

Blaine pulled the Spencer .38 from its scabbard and moved the horses so he had a clear view of the buckskin and the saloon doorway. A long minute passed as he fidgeted and wiped one hand and then another on his pants. Then he jerked as a gunshot blasted inside the saloon. He levered a shell into the rifle as four more shots roared. A man came running out of the saloon, head down and bent forward with a pistol in his hand. It was Chip Fenwick. He leapt off the sidewalk and grabbed at the buckskin's reins. The horse was pulling backward and tightening the slip-knot.

"Hold it right there," said Blaine.

Fenwick spun around, and his eyes widened. "It's you!" He raised his pistol and pointed.

Blaine was sure that for an instant, Fenwick thought he was seeing Tom again. But it didn't matter. Blaine pulled the trigger and put a .38 slug through Chip Fenwick's mid-section.

The small man snapped backwards, hit the hitching rail, and tried to hook it with his arm as he fell to the ground. His six-gun spilled in the dirt, and his hat rolled into the street. The buckskin had broken the reins and was off on a gallop.

Potter appeared at the dark doorway, holding his pistol down by his knee. A red stain colored his shirt. He raised his head as if to say something, and then he fell face forward onto the sidewalk.

Blaine stood with the rifle in his hands, waiting to see if anyone came out of the saloon. A minute later, a bare-headed man with a shotgun came around the corner of the building.

"Don't think about shootin' again," he said. "This'll cut you in two."

"Are you the law?"

"I don't have to be. I own this saloon. What the hell do you men think you're doing, comin' in here and shootin' everything to bits?"

"I shot to keep from gettin' killed." Blaine pointed with his rifle. "This man here has a reward out for him. And that man is a bounty hunter. Or was."

"And you?"

"I came looking for my brother. But he's not here."

"Well, I don't like any of you." The man with the shotgun turned. "What is it, Elliot?"

A young, thin, pale man stepped out of the saloon onto the sidewalk, leaning on a cane. His hair was cut short all the way around, and his pale blue eyes flickered from side to side. "Timothy's dead, Gibb."

"Son of a bitch. How did it happen? I was in back."

"This stranger come up to the table where Timothy and the other one was talkin'. All of a sudden they started shootin'."

"Who shot first?"

The nervous man nodded toward Fenwick's body. "I think the little fella did."

"This is a hell of a mess." Gibb looked at the two bodies and then at Blaine. "Do you mean to collect the bounty on this one?"

"No, someone else can have it. His name's Chip Fenwick, and he's wanted in Kansas. Robbery and jailbreak. Tell 'em you found him with Ed Timothy, and it might help. The other one's name is Potter, by the way."

"And your brother? You said you're lookin' for him?"

"Not any more. I know where he is." Blaine looked across the shimmering plains to the south, where the tips of the Dettman Buttes were barely visible. Like Potter said, Tom wasn't going anywhere. If there was anything good about this, it was the knowledge that Tom's body wouldn't be dug up and brought in by a bounty hunter. Blaine took a deep breath and fought the tightness in his throat. He could stop there on his way back and say good-bye.

Night Falls at Lonetree

Rob Ellman stood by his horse in the willow thicket, holding the reins close and peering out at the dry country he had just ridden across. The incident had been way too close for comfort, and although he had not recognized the man who came upon him in his work, he was sure the man had gotten a good look at him. He had been in such a hurry to get out of the place that he had left his rope on the calf and his running iron by the small sagebrush fire. Now his mouth was dry and his heart was still pounding, and he wondered if his horse could smell his fear.

He knew what he had to do. He had to break with the Red Sash boys, and he had to convince May he was done with all of it. He knew she would believe him because he knew that at last he believed it himself. He did not want to be a rustler any more.

He had said it before, but he had not felt it as he did now. It had been one of those things he found easy to put off—tomorrow, next week, as soon as he had enough jingle. But there was no waiting now. He was done with the lariat trail, and he just hoped it wasn't too late to get out.

He took slow, deliberate breaths to try to steady himself. The horse was breathing even now, too, and Ellman could hear the flowing of the creek.

He moved his hand down the reins and led the horse to the flowing water. Crouching upstream from the animal, he cupped his hands and washed his face. The water of Galena Creek was not as clear as that of a mountain stream, but he could see the silty bottom. He wet his lips, took a mouthful from his cupped hands, and spit it out. It was not much better than ditch water. He would wait for a real drink when he got to camp.

After another long look through the screen of willows, Ellman led the dark horse out into the open and mounted up. Keeping to low country, he struck a course through the rolling hills and headed northwest to the Baxter Buttes.

* * * * *

The first to meet him in camp was Dinsmore, whose troubled expression told him that bad news had gotten there ahead of him.

Ellman dismounted and said, "Nothin' good, huh?"

Dinsmore, who was light-haired and slender and had an easy way about him, shrugged and said, "Not today."

Ellman led his horse to the brush corral, where he turned the animal in without stripping the saddle and bridle. Then he walked toward the fire pit in front of the main tent, where the other men had gathered. No one had built an evening fire yet.

Russ Wilt stood aside from the others and waited for Ellman to approach. The rustler boss had a high chest and a thick frame, and he stood with his chin lifted. He did not miss a chance to throw around his authority.

"Where's your rope?" he asked.

"I didn't have time to get it."

143

Wilt's eyes narrowed, and small flecks of spit flew in the air as he said, "Stupid. You get caught red-handed."

"It could happen to anyone."

"It happened to you. Because you were stupid. I told every one of you we had to be careful, and you go out and get seen. Who was it?"

"I don't know."

"Well, I'll tell you. There's three guesses. If it was a cattleman, he would have gone to take the rope off the calf. If it was a lawman, he would have chased you, maybe taken a shot. If it was Sexton, he would have shot and not missed."

"No one shot at me. Who's Sexton?"

"He's the one the cattlemen brought in. He's already picked off a couple of others, and talk is, we're on his list, once he gets us identified."

"I didn't know they brought someone in."

"I told you to be careful, didn't I? And you blunder right along."

That was the man's way, Ellman thought. Never tell any more than he had to, not even to his own men. Ellman looked at the other two by the fire pit, Face and Orson. Then he spoke to Wilt. "Seems like the news of my blunder got back ahead of me."

"Probably half the people in the country know it by now. Man on a dark horse throws down his long rope and runs for his life."

"If everyone knows so much, why don't you know who saw me?"

"Because, stupid, the man who saw you didn't boil up a cloud of dust clear across the country."

Ellman looked again at Face and Orson. He was sure that one of them had told the boss, but it didn't matter. The news was out, and even if Wilt was exaggerating how many people knew it, the incident wasn't going to go away by itself.

The boss spoke again. "From now on, the only work you do is at night."

Ellman glanced around at the other men. Dinsmore had joined the group but stood a couple of paces to the side. With all four present, Ellman knew the moment had come for him to say what he had to.

"I don't know that I want to do any more work at all. Not of this kind."

Wilt's eyes narrowed again. "What do you mean?"

Ellman took a deep breath and tried to speak in an even tone. "What I mean is, I don't want to be a Red Sash rider any more."

Silence fell. No one in the group wore an actual red sash, but they used the name as a code. Only those within the ring knew that they called themselves the Red Sash outfit, and if Ellman left, he would take that knowledge with him. He would also take a knowledge of everything the Red Sashers had done.

Wilt broke the silence. "What makes you think you want to get out?"

"Well, it's evident that none of you like the way things have gotten complicated."

"All the more reason for you to stay in, shut up, and not be seen."

Ellman shook his head. "No, I've had it. I made my mind up when I was hiding out this afternoon, and I know what I've got to do."

"You don't know as much as you think," said Orson. He was bearded and burly, and even though the group didn't have a formal order, he acted as second in command.

Ellman faced him. "I know about me," he said, "and I'm done with all of this."

"You mean you're a coward," said Orson.

Ellman knew he was being called out, but he brushed aside the challenge. "That's what you mean. I'm trying to use judgment. So save it."

Wilt came back into the conversation. "And your judgment tells you to run, just like you did this afternoon. In plain view of everyone."

"Call it what you will," said Ellman, "but I'm clearing out." He walked toward the smaller tent that he and Dinsmore shared. Once inside, he rolled his blankets and made sure his personal effects were all in his duffel bag.

Stepping outside, he saw Wilt standing in the open with his hand near his gun and holster.

"You're not going anywhere, Ellman," said the boss.

"You'll have to shoot me in the back, with your other men watching." Ellman turned and walked toward the corral. He carried his bedroll under his left arm and his duffel bag in his hand, with both objects between him and Wilt.

"Stop!" hollered the boss.

Ellman heard the click of a gun. Tossing the bag and bedroll to his left, he fell to his right and drew his gun as he turned. Wilt's pistol roared, and the bullet split the air above Ellman's head. Before Wilt could adjust his aim, Ellman fired at the man's mid-section.

The rustler boss spun a quarter of the way around, dropping his gun and then falling onto his left side. "Get him!" he rasped.

Ellman came up in a crouch with his gun leveled. None of the other three men moved. "I'm leaving," he said. "I didn't ask to be shot at, and if anyone else tries it, I'll shoot again."

He gathered up his bag and bedroll, and within five minutes he had his gear tied onto his horse and was riding out of the Red Sash camp.

Night was falling as he left the Baxter Butte country and headed again for Galena Creek. He realized he had not filled his canteen at the spring where the Red Sashers had their camp, and he did not have any grub. That was all right, he told himself. He could drink from the creek. He would worry about food tomorrow, and after that he would see what he could do about getting a change of horses. For right now he was alive, and he needed to stay that way.

* * * * *

The first human being he saw the next day was Dinsmore. The lean, light-haired rider was ambling along on his sorrel horse when Ellman stepped out of the willows and gave a whistle.

Dinsmore jerked his head up and around, then turned his horse toward the creek.

"How bad are things now?" asked Ellman.

"Not good."

"Is Wilt still alive?"

"Yes, he is, but he's none the better for what happened yesterday evening." After a pause, Dinsmore added, "He gave orders for us to shoot you on sight."

"Thanks for not followin' through. I doubt Orson or Face will be so considerate."

"They're clearly on his side, but you're not the only thing they've got to worry about."

"Is that right?"

Dinsmore tipped back his hat and glanced around. "Oh, yeah. Wilt was serious when he said this fella Sexton is workin' his way through the list."

Ellman frowned. "I don't even know him. What's he look like?"

"I haven't seen him, either, but they say he's a pale one with yella hair, almost white. Rides a dark grey horse, dresses in the same color. Hardly ever comes close. Carries a field glass and a Winchester with one of them telescopic sights."

Ellman felt a chill across the back of his shoulders. "You don't know what part of the country he's workin' right now?"

Dinsmore shook his head. "Got a few people worried, though."

"I guess." Ellman saw that Dinsmore was scanning the country, so he said, "Don't let me keep you. Thanks, though, for the warning."

"Think nothing of it. In fact, I wasn't even here." Dinsmore pulled his dove-colored hat down to his brow and rode away.

* * * * *

Ellman followed the creek on foot, leading the horse and picking his way through the willows and box elders. The sun was hot, and the air was close. Gnats buzzed around his head and moved in a cloud above the dark horse. After a couple of miles, Ellman led the horse out of the cover of trees and into the open air, where a faint breeze gave the illusion of freedom.

Off to the north, Ellman saw a pine ridge running from east to west. Halfway between the creek and the ridge was a place called Lonetree Station. He needed to cross about four miles of open ground to get there.

Even an open stretch of country had dips and rises, with an occasional washout or low bluff where someone could be hiding. But Ellman knew he had to take the chance. He mounted the horse and set out on a lope, altering his course every few hundred yards but keeping north.

The lone cedar tree and the clump of buildings came into view, disappeared as he rode into a low spot, and showed again as he covered the last half-mile.

He tied the dark horse at the hitching rail and went inside, where the dim interior made him pause to adjust his eyes. A large, heavy man with a balding head stood behind the counter, where he was sorting a pile of beans on a table top. At the end of the same table, a tired-looking woman was mixing ingredients in a bread pan.

"What can I do for you?" asked the man.

"Could use something to eat."

"If you want to eat right away, there's yesterday's bread and cold beef."

"That sounds fine." Ellman sat at a table and waited as the man brought him half a round loaf of bread and about a pound of what looked like shoulder meat.

As Ellman dug in, the man brought a cup and a coffee pot and set them on the table.

"Coffee's not very hot," said the man, "but it drinks."

Ellman had his meal in silence. When he was done, he walked to the counter and laid down two bits. "Will this cover it, Fred?"

The man looked up with blank eyes. "We don't know you," he said.

"That's fine. Chances are, I haven't been here before, and I don't expect to come in again."

The man's eyebrows moved, and he went back to sorting beans.

Outside, Ellman took his horse to the shady side of the stable and stood looking out over the austere country. After a few minutes, he heard a soft voice.

"Hello, Rob."

He turned to his left and saw her, soft and blonde and light, stepping from sunshine into shade.

"Hello, May. I can't tell you how much good it does me to see you."

"I'm glad to see you, too," she said, but she did not move close.

He smiled. Then he said, "I've come to tell you that I'm makin' a change."

She did not look straight up as she said, "I heard Mr. Ward tell Mrs. Ward that you were on the run."

"That's one way of puttin' it. Another way is that I'm goin' straight." As he saw her blank expression, he added, "Not that what I was doin' was all that crooked. All I ever did was mavericks. I never changed a brand. But even that much is in my past. I broke with the rest of the boys last night. They didn't like it, but I'm on my own."

Worry came into her eyes. "What are you going to do, Rob?"

"I've got to lay low until I can get a different horse. Then I'll come for you."

Her face had gone expressionless again.

"Don't you want to go?" he asked.

"Well, yes, I suppose."

"You said before that you wanted to get out of this place more than anything in the world, and that you'll go with me."

"I know I said that, and I'm not saying I won't now."

"But—"

"But nothing, Rob."

"There's something."

"Well, I guess there is. I just don't know about living like that, where you feel that there's someone always after you."

"I'm changing that," he said. "I won't come for you unless there's no one after me. That's fair, isn't it?"

Her blue eyes were moist as she said, "I guess so."

"Well, be on the lookout for me. If it's not tonight, it'll be tomorrow night."

"And if you don't come?"

"I will. You can count on it."

"Oh, Rob." Now she came to him and buried her face in his shirt front, between his chest and shoulder.

He patted her on the back of the head and said, "Don't worry. I'll be all right, and I'll come back for you."

* * * * *

The afternoon shadows were growing as Ellman watched from his hiding place along the creek. He had decided to try his luck with a horse trader named Jimmie Franklin, who had a place about halfway between Lonetree Station and the Baxter Buttes. As soon as the shadows stretched out a little more, he would set off for Jimmie's place.

Ellman watered his horse and walked it back and forth in a small open area between the box elder trees and the creek. Then he checked the cinch, turned out the stirrup, and swung aboard. *Here goes*, he said to himself.

For the first mile, the country was flat and he saw no one. Then he began to cross gullies and go around low outcroppings. He paused at the edge of a broad, grassy basin, where he would be in the open for half a mile if he cut across. As he studied the layout, he squinted. Either way he went, he could run into bad luck, so he couldn't let himself think too much about consequences. He went straight north.

When he had gotten out to the middle of the basin, he flinched at the sight of a horse and rider coming down from the breaks on his left. As the rider came out of the shadows, however, Ellman was relieved to see that it was Dinsmore. The dove-colored hat and light hair bobbed in the late afternoon as the sorrel came loping.

Ellman reined his horse to a stop and waited until Dinsmore pulled up.

"Didn't expect to see you again so soon," Ellman said. "What's new?"

The slender rider seemed to be trying to catch his breath. "Face and Orson," he said. "Not a mile behind me. Can't let 'em see me talkin' to you. You need to make a run for it."

Before Ellman could say a word in answer, Dinsmore stiffened as if in shock. He fell to his left side as the boom of a rifle carried across the open area. Dinsmore tumbled to the ground, and his horse bolted in a run.

Ellman swung down from the dark horse and pulled on the reins to keep the animal from rearing and twisting away. With the horse at his left, he knelt beside Dinsmore.

The young rider was already dead, shot through the back. Face and Orson were nowhere in sight, so the shot must have come from the breaks about four hundred yards to the southwest. As Ellman crouched, wondering about his next move, the dark horse lurched and squealed, then toppled over as the crash of rifle fire rolled across the basin.

Ellman lay flat on the ground next to the dying horse, which was heaving and gasping. He hoped the animal would shield him from the sniper, but even at that, he knew he wouldn't last long if the sharpshooter changed position. He guessed it was Sexton, but whoever it was, the man had deadly aim.

A long five minutes passed. Ellman kept his eye on the place where he thought the shots came from, but he saw no movement. That didn't mean much. The man could drop back and, depending on the lay of the land, ride halfway around the basin and keep out of sight. The next shot could come from anywhere.

The dark horse expired with a long groan and a thrashing of the legs. Ellman looked around and saw no sign of Dinsmore's sorrel. It was probably still running with the reins trailing and the stirrups flopping.

A few more minutes passed, and then two riders emerged from the breaks where Dinsmore had come from. It had to be Face and Orson. They were heading straight for the spot where Ellman lay by the dead horse, not far from Dinsmore's body. Ellman pulled at the stock of his rifle, but the weight of the horse sank too flat on the scabbard for him to budge the gun.

The two riders kept coming. It was Face and Orson, all right. If they had heard the shots, which they probably had, they would think the gunfire had been exchanged right here. They were coming to clean up.

This was it, Ellman thought. If the sharpshooter didn't get him, these other two would. If there was any way he could talk to them first, get them to join with him and turn on Sexton—but they had their pistols drawn and were riding straight at him.

He could see Face's yellow teeth and Orson's dark beard. The riders were no more than fifty yards away when the melee started. Face pitched forward, slumped against his saddle horn, and slipped to the left as the report of the rifle came crashing. Ellman jumped up and sprang toward the horse, a wild-eyed bay that was plunging and bucking. As Ellman grabbed for the reins, the horse cut to the left and charged away. Face rolled to the ground, lifeless, and Ellman drew his gun.

Orson came riding straight at him where he stood. The man held his six-gun at arm's length, trying to level his aim on Ellman.

Another rifle shot tore the air, but for once the sniper seemed to have missed. It caused the horse to cut sharp, though, and Orson's hand was wavering as he tried to find his target again.

Ellman jumped aside and came up on the horse's left. Now Orson had to raise his pistol up and over the horse's mane, and as he did so, Ellman sent a bullet through the burly man's ribs. This time when Ellman grabbed for the rein, he caught it.

As Orson spilled off to the right side, Ellman grabbed both reins and pulled the horse around straight. It was a medium-sized brown horse, obedient, and when it planted both front feet in a standstill, Ellman tossed the reins into place and swung into the saddle. In another couple of seconds he was on a dead run to the north.

Not until he reached the broken country on the other side of the basin did he realize he had left behind all his worldly possessions—his saddle, rifle, duffel bag, and bedroll. He had gotten a change of horses, as it turned out, but at no small price.

Taking cover behind a low bluff, he dismounted and found a lookout spot. He kept a firm grip on the reins as he watched the scene where the bodies of three men and a horse lay strewn. He wondered why the sharpshooter had not shot at him when he was riding away, and he figured it was either because the man didn't have him identified or because, having missed once, he did not want to take another bad shot. Ellman mulled it over as he continued to wait and watch.

After a while, a rider came out of the breaks in the southwest. He was riding a dark grey horse and was dressed in the same leaden hue. When he reached the middle of the grassy basin, he drew his pistol, then reined his horse around and craned his neck as he gave the bodies a looking over. With his inspection finished, he stopped his horse and put away his gun. Raising his head, he cast a long glance to the north, in the direction where Ellman was hiding but not at the very spot.

The fading afternoon sun illumined the man's pale face and whitish hair. From this distance it was hard to guess his age, but Ellman had the illusion that he was a hundred years old and would never die. If he came this way, Ellman would have to try to shoot him, and he didn't know if he had the nerve to make a steady shot.

The assassin must have known better than to ride into possible ambush. He turned his horse to the southwest, where he
had come from, and took off on a lope. Ellman watched the
moving object until it disappeared into the shadows of the
breaks a mile away.

With Orson's rope tied to the saddle horn, Ellman got his
own saddle free, along with the rifle, bedroll, and duffel bag.
He made short work of transferring his gear onto the brown
horse. He left the extra saddle and blanket where they lay,
and he draped Orson's bridle on top. He untied the rope from
the saddle horn and gave it a few seconds' thought as he gathered it. A man always needed one of these, and his was gone.
Then he shook his head and dropped the coiled rope on the
ground next to the dead man's saddle.

He led the brown horse out a few steps, checked his cinch,
and mounted up. The horse moved at an easy lope as Ellman
headed north again.

* * * * *

Dusk was gathering as he approached Lonetree Station from
the west. A dull light showed in one of the windows, and
movement sounded from within the stable as horses shifted in
the stalls. Ellman rode around to the front of the station, and
seeing no horses tied at the rail, he dismounted and stood in
the yard. The door of the roadhouse was open, but Ellman
could see no one.

He had told himself over and over that the Wards had no
claim on the girl. She worked for them of her own free will.

Yet he did not know what he would do if Ward came out and told him to move along, that the girl did not want to see him.

The people inside had to know he was here. After all, they ran a way station, and it was their business to hear footfalls, spurs, and bit chains. If Ward did not come to the door, it was a good sign.

Ellman waited. The brown horse shook his saddle. A low voice inside muttered a few words, and another voice answered. Ellman heard movement, and following the sound, he saw a faint shadow travel in the dim light. Then a form appeared at the doorway, and May stepped outside.

"Rob," she said in a soft voice as she came toward him.

"I came like I said I would."

She stopped about four feet away. "I was afraid for you."

"I'm all right. There was a scrape, but I came out of it." When she didn't move or speak, he added, "Nobody's after me. I'm on my own, and I'm headin' for new country."

"I'm glad for you, Rob."

"I'm goin' to make a new start, like I told you." He moistened his lips. "I hope you can come with me."

She did not answer.

His heart started beating faster now, not with the same fear as before but with a fear nonetheless. "What's the matter, May? Don't you want to go with me?"

Night was drawing in so that he could barely see the features of her face, but her tears glistened as she said, "It's not that I don't want to."

"What is it, then? They can't keep you."

"I know."

His eyebrows tightened. "Then what is it?"

"Oh, Rob," she said, with a cry in her voice. "It's not that I don't want to, or I can't, but that I know, deep down, that I shouldn't."

His hands fell to his sides. "But, May—"

"I'm sorry, Rob."

"Then—that's it?"

Her voice was steadier now as she said, "You will always be in my heart, Rob, and we have had special times together, but I know I shouldn't do this thing."

He clung to his hope. "Even if I make a new start."

"I pray that you do. But you have to make it over all the way. For your own sake as well as mine."

"You think that what I've done will always come between us, then."

"It would follow us, even if no one else did."

He felt his spirits sink again. "And you don't know if I can really change."

"I hope you can. But only you will know."

He was putting together all she had said. She had not wavered, and she must have had it thought out ahead of time. "I guess that's it," he said at last. "Just remember, May, that I love you, and I have tried."

"I know you have."

He realized she did not say in return that she loved him. He could have gotten it out of her, but instead he said, "Goodbye, May." His throat tightened, and he had no more to say. He moved his right hand along the reins as he got ready to turn and leave.

"Good-bye, Rob. And be careful."

He led the brown horse away into the darkness, and he did not look back as he mounted up. After a deep breath, he touched his spur to the horse and headed north.

He told himself he was lucky, for he had escaped the bullet and the noose. He told himself to accept that much, to be thankful he was alive and free. He told himself he would prove he could do better when he made a new start in the next place. He had to tell himself all those things over and over as he rode through the long, dark night.

Song of Pierre

I was sitting in the shade of the water trough on the main street of Bonnet when Cactus Pete came riding up on his wall-eyed roan. The horse looked like buzzard meat just waiting for its destiny. Its head hung low, and its hipbones stuck out so that a man could have hung his hat on one side and a rope on the other. Cactus Pete didn't look much better, except that for a desert rat he had something of a belly. It sloped down from his chest and out in front so that it touched his saddle horn, and if he had been a cook he could have rolled out a pie crust on it.

With a heave he got his right leg up and over, then slid down off the saddle. I knew who he was, but I hadn't seen him up close before. Now I did as he looked down at me. He wore a battered hat, and beneath that he had thick brows, yellowed eyes, and a dark, bushy beard. When he opened his mouth, I saw that he had about half his teeth left.

"You're the kid named Dinky, aren't ya?"

I stood up and shielded my eyes from the sun. "I sure am."

"Ha-ha," he said. "Come on, now, bitch."

I realized he was talking to the horse, not only because of the tone of his voice but because he was elbowing it in the chest as the horse pushed against him.

Pete's bleary eyes came back to me as he let the horse drink. "They say you do a little work now and then."

"When I can."

He looked me over. "Meanin' you're not big enough to do some things?"

"I guess." I was fourteen years old, almost fifteen, but I wasn't five feet tall yet, and I weighed less than a hundred pounds.

"That's enough for now." He jerked on the reins, and the horse's head came up with its muzzle dripping. Pete turned to me with a relaxed smile. "Don't let 'em drink too much at one time." Then he gave me a close look and said, "I don't need a big kid for this job. Someone about your size should be all right." He lifted his hat the way people do to let the air cool the sweat. After a couple of seconds he tipped his head back and wrinkled his nose. "Got to get you somethin' to cover your noggin, though."

"I've got a cap."

"Well, you need to get it. Towheads like you turn red and like to die in the sun."

I frowned. "I don't know what kind of job it is yet."

He gave a backward wave of his hand. "Ah, don't worry. It ain't nothin' illegal or immoral. I just need someone to go through a hole that I can't git through." He patted his belly. Then he stretched out his mouth so that his beard moved, and he said, "You've not got anyone to answer to, eh? They say you're an orflin'."

That was me, the boy who did odd jobs. I did some work at the livery stable, where I had a cot in the harness room. But I came and went as I pleased, and no one in Bonnet seemed to take much notice. "That's right," I said. "I'm all on my own."

"Nothin' wrong with that."

I squinted at the sun and thought about what he had said about towheads. "Where is it?"

"Where's what?"

"The hole?"

I guess I spoke too loud. He tightened his face, and his hand moved as if he wanted to grab my chin. Then he looked around, drew his hand back to his hip, and said, "You don't need to go blabbin' it up and down the street."

With my voice lowered I said, "Well, where is it? This job."

His face relaxed as he settled his gaze on me. "A little bit more than a day's ride out. Be gone three days, four at the most. Good pay, too."

"How much is that?"

"Two bits a day, and you eat good."

I twisted my mouth. "I can make four bits a day and not have to dodge rattlers in the desert."

"If all I had to worry about was rattlers—well, let me put it this way. One place is about the same as the next. Maybe you've got water and shade here, but you ride with Cactus Pete, and you learn to ration your water from a canteen and sit in the shade of your horse. Make a man out of ya."

I looked at the crowbait roan. "Do you have a horse for me?"

"Oh, no. You don't get a horse. You'll ride Pierre."

"Who's he?"

"My burro. Just right for the likes of you."

* * * * *

My idea of a burro was a sand-colored fella with maybe a stripe down his back, but Pierre turned out to be a husky, black critter with coarse hair like buffalo wool. I had seen black donkeys before, of course, but I had never paid much attention to any of them, and just looking at Pierre took some getting used to. His head and neck made up a third of his size, and the area between his eyes looked like a person could use it for an anvil.

As Pete held the lead rope, I moved forward to touch Pierre. He shied away as if he didn't trust me, and I thought that made us even. I didn't know much about burros, but I had already made up my mind that I wasn't going to let him bite me or kick me if I could help it.

Pete handed me the hemp rope and said, "Go ahead and git on."

The rope came down from a hackamore, also made of hemp. I wondered if that was all I was going to have. "No saddle?" I asked.

"Don't need one. Just grab a hank of hair and climb on."

Well, I'd gotten onto bareback horses a lot taller than this donkey, but I didn't think it was going to be the same. With my left hand I held the rope and grabbed Pierre's mane, which stuck out about three inches. I planted my right hand on his backbone, but as soon as I tried to push myself up, Pierre sash-ayed away from me.

I tried it a couple of more times, and we came around full circle.

Pete said, "Hell's fire," and he grabbed me by the neck of my shirt and the seat of my pants and slung me up onto Pierre's back.

The smelly little beast took off running, and then his long black ears went down. His hips came up in back of me, and I pitched forward to the right. The ground came up with a wallop, harder than I had ever been socked on the jaw. I still had the rope, though, and it threw Pierre off balance. He hit the dirt with a grunt, and his four little hooves went up in the air.

"That's good," said Pete. "You hang on for dear life. Last thing you want is to be bucked off in the middle of the desert and be left on foot."

I got up and brushed the dirt from my face. "You'll be there to help me, won't you?"

"Oh, sure. But I mean for general purposes. You learn somethin' now you can use for the rest of your life. Don't forget to pick up your cap. It gets hot out there, you know."

* * * * *

The first night on the trail, I found out what Cactus Pete meant by eating good. I got my own can of beans, which I ate cold, using the folded can lid as my spoon.

As the night got chilly, I asked him why we didn't have a fire.

"One," he said, "there ain't a hell of a lot to burn out here, except a few sticks of brush. And two, I don't like to attract rattlers."

"Oh, do snakes come to a fire?"

"The kind I'm thinkin' of do."

He got up and walked in the direction of where he'd left the roan mare tied. Thirty yards away, in the opposite direction, I could make out Pierre's dark shape where he grazed at the end of his rope. With no warning he raised his head and let out a piercing, wheezing, grating *wunh-hunh* sound that sent a chill across my shoulders.

Pete's voice came across the evening air. "Aw, shaddup, you fool." When he came to sit on his saddle, he said, "You see why they call 'em canaries. Them an' mules. Hell of a song to wake up to in the mornin'."

I looked past Pierre into the darkness of the desert. "If there was that other kind of rattlesnake out there, wouldn't they hear him?"

Pete wrinkled his nose and wiped the back of his hand across it. "I kinda forgot about that part earlier. Can't think of everything at once." He sniffed.

Pierre sang again. *Wunh-hunh, wunh-hunh, wunh-hunh-hunh.*

I said, "I guess you get used to it."

"Oh, you can get used to just about anything if you live long enough."

* * * * *

Sure enough, Pierre's song had me awake long before daylight. It brought me out of sleep and the world of dreams to the hard ground where I lay curled up under my sarape.

Pete made a thump as he shifted under his blankets. "Git up and take them animals to water, boy."

"All the way back there?" We had stopped at a waterhole the evening before and then come about two miles further until we pitched camp. Pete had said that was the way to do things in the desert—let other animals drink, and avoid bad company. Now I wondered.

"Ha-ha," came his voice. "Just a joke. But we'd better git up and at it, cover as much ground as we can before the sun starts scorchin'."

Within a few minutes we had our camp picked up, and Pete went to fetch his horse. When he came back, I asked if we were going to eat anything.

"You take the sun better if you haven't ate too much," he said. "We'll eat good when we get back. Here, hold this rope."

As Pete went to work brushing the roan with his hand, Pierre held his head straight out from his shoulders and started braying.

"Give me that rope," said Pete, "and go untie that fool so he'll shut up. We got things to do."

When I came back with Pierre, Pete had slung on the blankets and saddle and was pulling the cinch strap. It was weathered and cracked, and I was afraid it would break with Pete's weight leaning back on it, but everything stayed in place. The roan gave out a short breath, then stood with her head hung as Pete picked up each of her four feet and looked at the undersides. After that he handed me the rope and took the bridle off the saddle horn. In another minute he had the headstall latched and the rope coiled.

"Don't crowd me," he said to the horse. He pushed her sideways, then led her out a few steps. He went to the saddle again, fingered the cinch, and turned out the stirrup. When he heaved himself aboard, the mare let out a long, tired breath. Pete reined around. "Git on. Time's a-wastin'."

After the previous day on the trail, Pierre and I had an understanding. He let me get on, but it was up to me to stay on and get straightened up as he took off on a jiggling trot. So I hung onto his mane and wrestled my way into place as we followed Pete and the skinny roan into the desert.

We traveled northwest, like the day before. At late morning we came to a line of hills that ran east and west. Pete came to a stop about half a mile away. His eyes roved back and forth, and I imagined he was looking for a place in the hillside where there was a hole for a boy like me to crawl through. I had heard plenty of stories about old caves and hidden gold and all that, and I figured that as long as it wasn't a snake den, I could crawl in and crawl out, and we could go back and eat. I was getting hungry.

Pete seemed to have gotten his bearings. He reined his horse to the left, gigged her with his heels, and headed for a place where the chemise grew a little thicker than in the rest of the area around us.

At the edge of the patch of brush, Pete stopped and let me catch up. He looked all around, with his eyes narrow and hard.

"Git down and tie that donkey to a clump of this greasewood," he said. "Find one that's by itself, so he won't get wrapped up so bad."

I did as I was told. Meanwhile Pete tied up the skinny mare, who looked as if she was used to standing in the sun and getting her brains baked. She stood with her head in the bush as Pete untied another rope he had carried along on his saddle. I hadn't thought about it until now.

It was a grass rope like the others, nearly an inch thick. When he tossed it out to uncoil it, I saw that it was about fifty feet long.

"What's that for?" I asked.

"Why, to let you down."

"What?"

"And bring you back up, of course."

I looked around at the baked dirt and clumps of brush. "What kind of a hole is this?"

"Why, it's a hole in the ground. What did you think?"

I ran my tongue across my lips. "I guess it doesn't matter much. I was expecting a cave."

He began coiling the rope again. "Come on."

With Pierre wheezing and honking behind me, I followed Pete through the brush. We came to a place where a heap of debris sat in an open spot with chemise all around. Thin, dead branches lay in a kind of a mat, with tumbleweeds stuck where they had been driven by the wind.

"That's it," said Pete. "We need to clear that stuff out of the way."

I stared at the heap, thinking how I wouldn't be surprised to find an Indian buried beneath it.

"Well, get started." Pete's voice got bossy, and I realized "we" meant me.

I started dragging away the branches and shaking off the tumbleweeds. After a few minutes I saw the wrinkle of a tattered piece of canvas, and when I pulled away the last of the brush, the canvas sank in the middle and dropped down into a hole. A little cloud of dead particles hovered over the opening.

I could see now why Pete had brought me. The hole was about a foot and a half across, and trying to get him through it would be like trying to get a potato into a whiskey bottle. I thought I could fit through it, but I sure didn't like the idea.

I turned to look at Pete, who held out a loop at the end of his rope.

"Put this around your waist."

"What are you going to tie it to?"

"Don't have to. I'll let you down, hand over hand, and I'll put my weight against it if I need to."

My eyes went to the hole. "How deep is it?"

"Not much. Twenty, twenty-five feet."

I jerked around, and I almost bumped into him, as he had stepped forward and was raising the loop to put it down over my head.

"I don't know," I said. "This isn't what I thought."

Now he grabbed me by the chin, like I thought he was going to do a couple of days earlier at the water trough. He held his thumb against my right jaw and his fingers against my left. His grip was strong and rough.

"Now look here, kid. We didn't come all this way to get weak in the knees at this point. You've got a job to do, and when you get it done, we'll pull out of here and beat it back to the settlements."

I sagged. "What am I supposed to look for?"

"Why, gold. Did you think we came out here to look for marbles?"

"No, but what kind of gold?"

"Coins."

"Are they in something?"

"There should be four leather pouches. When you find 'em, give me one tug on the rope. I'll toss you down a gunny sack, and you can put 'em all in the sack and tie it onto the end of the rope. Then you give me two tugs, and I'll pull it up."

"Why don't I give you two tugs, and I hang onto the rope above the sack, and you pull us up together?"

His eyes opened. "Don't you trust old Cactus Pete?"

"It's not that, but—"

"Oh, hell. That's all right. I'll pull you up together."

"What if I don't find anything?"

"Well, you should. But if you don't, just tug 'er twice anyway, and I'll pull you up. I hope it don't turn out that way, though, 'cause it took me a lot of trouble to find out where this stash was. So don't give up if you don't find it the first minute you're down there. You look around real good."

"I will."

He raised the loop up over my head, and I got it down around my chest with my arms over it. We walked to the hole, where I got down on all fours, lowered my feet into the darkness, and grabbed the rope for dear life. Pete leaned over and smiled, and I got a close-up view of his dark beard and yellow teeth. Then his grimy hands fed the rope forward and let me down into the pit. The rope grazed the side of the opening and sent a shower of dirt into my face, so I shut my eyes and turned aside. When I looked up again, I saw a circle of pale blue sky. Cactus Pete was out of view, and only the rope and the song of Pierre connected me to the world up on top.

When I hit the bottom, the first thing I stepped on was the rumpled canvas. It gave me a creepy feeling until I realized what it was. The light was pretty dim at the bottom of the hole, but my eyes adjusted and I could see I was in something like a cave. I took the rope off and moved around, peering in the darkness and feeling with my feet. It seemed like a tunnel led back into the mountain, but I didn't know how far back in there to look, and I thought I should ask Pete for a candle and some matches. So I went to the rope and gave it two tugs.

I was barely done with the second tug when the rope came slithering down like a big snake, coming straight at me and throwing more dirt in my face. I jumped aside, and the rope fell in a pile at my feet.

I hollered upwards. "Pete! Pete!"

A shape crossed over the small circle of light up above, but no face appeared at the edge.

I squinted with my head tipped back, and I heard a *Pop! Pop!*

I hollered again. "Pete!"

Now a figure appeared at the top of the hole, and it looked like someone reaching his hand down. The blast of a gun and the concussion of air made me jump back into the cave. Two more shots roared in the narrow hole. I moved back up against the far wall.

I had no idea of what was going on up on top, but I tried to figure it out. I was sure of one thing. Cactus Pete had every reason in the world not to be shooting at me, just as he had every reason not to let go of the rope. That meant someone else was shooting, probably the same person who made the first two popping sounds. As I imagined the scene up on top, things didn't look very good for Cactus Pete.

They didn't look good for me, either. My first worry was that someone was going to come down and shoot me, but after some thought I talked myself out of that idea. Anyone even a little bigger than I was would not be able to come down that hole. It would be much easier just to leave me down there. And even if someone did let down another rope, I didn't know if I wanted to be pulled up to meet him. Not after those gun-shots.

So I figured I was going to have to find another way out. I turned and made my way to the passageway I had found a few minutes earlier. I groped with my hands and took small steps forward as I made my way farther into the dark. I gave one last thought toward Cactus Pete and the donkey Pierre up on top, and I concentrated on feeling my way back under the hillside.

I moved at a slow pace, stumbling from time to time on a lump of earth or on a rock that moved. I lost my sense of time, and I remembered a story the teacher had read to the class when I was still in school a couple of years earlier. It was about a man whose sweetheart had died and he got locked in her vault when the funeral was over. I think it was in France. In order to stay alive, he decided he was going to have to eat the two candles he found. He cut each one in half and allowed himself to eat half a candle every so often, like every twelve hours. So he waited the time out, and after he ate the last piece of candle, he was getting desperate. Then the girl's family realized he was missing, and they came back and opened the vault. He had turned all grey and hollow-eyed, and he asked how long he had been locked up with the dead girl. They told him he had been there an hour.

So I decided not to try to figure the time. I just walked, like a blind person with no cane, feeling with my hands and feet, wondering if the only way out was another long, narrow hole up to the surface.

It seemed to me that the passageway made a broad curve to the left, but I couldn't be sure, not any more than I could know how long I was in the dark or how far I shuffled and groped. At some point, though, the darkness was not so thick. I picked up my feet and took bigger steps, and in a little while I saw light filtering in. I moved faster, and I could see that the tunnel did curve. Then I saw the full light pouring in through the opening where the tunnel ended.

I walked out onto a hillside of brush and rocks. Not far below, a green valley spread out. A row of trees wandered through the middle, and a stream sparkled through the branches. The sight cheered me up, and I wanted to run down the hill. I was hungry and thirsty, but I made myself be careful. I remembered all too well how someone had tried to shoot me when I was down in the hole.

I stood on the hillside and studied the country all around me until my eyes ached. The sun was high and warm, not too hot, and I had my cap pulled down to my eyebrows, but the brightness of the outside world and the shimmering of the green valley were almost too much.

When my eyes relaxed and the surroundings started to seem normal, I began to walk down the hillside. I wouldn't have thought there was anything this green within five hundred miles of Bonnet, and I thought there had to be people around. I hoped they were friendly.

At the stream I took a long drink of water and washed my face. The water was cool and clear, and I could see the shiny pebbles in the bottom. The red, blue, black, grey, and white stones all looked new and perfect.

I wandered along the stream through the grass and trees. A light breeze rustled the leaves and brushed my face. The grass smelled fresh. I was getting hungrier every minute, and I wondered if any berries grew there.

I followed the stream where it curved around a rise in the land, and there in a grassy meadow I saw a camp, almost a town, of white tents. Light voices carried on the air.

I stopped at the edge of the trees, not sure whether I wanted to walk right into the camp. As I stood there, two boys came riding down the hillside on my left. They were riding ponies, a white one and a tan one. As they came closer, I saw that they both wore capes. They had long hair that came down over their ears but was well trimmed. They were both clean and smiling.

The one on the white pony called out in a cheerful voice. "Well, hello, boy. Are you lost?"

"I don't know."

He laughed. "Then you must be. But don't worry. Come on into our village."

"Don't be afraid," said the other boy. "I'll bet you're hungry."

I shrugged.

"Sure you are," said the first boy. "Come along. We'll ride ahead and let them know you're coming."

They galloped away through the grass, and I followed them toward the village of white tents.

Soon enough, I saw that all the tents were round. Just as surprising, everything was clean. As I walked along the main pathway with tents on each side, young people came to their doorways, or entryways, and smiled at me. Some said hello.

I followed the boys on ponies, who had stopped at a big, open tent and dismounted. Beneath the tent canopy, a long table was stocked with food, and two pretty girls sat on a bench next to it.

The boys tied their ponies to a tree and led me into the tent. "We have a visitor," said the boy who had been riding the white pony. He had brown hair, blue eyes, and a friendly smile.

A blond-haired girl stood up. She was wearing a dress of one long piece of fabric, gathered at the waist. "Come and sit down," she said. "You must be hungry."

It took all I had to control myself. I saw a platter of grapes, loaves of cut bread, a block of cheese, and a cutting board with a roasted chunk of meat.

"I don't know," I said.

"Come." She took me by the hand and led me to the table.

The other girl, who had light brown hair and honey-colored eyes, set a plate in front of me. As she leaned forward, the top of her dress hung loose and I saw the soft mound of her booby. She looked at me and smiled.

"I'm Waneena," she said. "And this is Vanessa."

I guessed them to be about sixteen or seventeen, like the two boys.

"My name's Daniel," I said. I sure didn't want any of them to know I was called Dinky.

"Don't be shy," said Waneena. She moved the bread and the cheese close to me.

As I began to eat, Vanessa picked up a carving knife and cut off four thick slices from the roasted meat. She lifted them using the blade of the knife and her pretty fingertips, and she slid the pieces onto my plate.

The meat was warm to the taste. "Mutton?" I asked.

With a soft smile she said, "Lamb."

"It's good."

"We're glad you like it. We just ate before you got here, and there's still plenty, so go ahead."

When I was finished with the bread and cheese and meat, the boys came around and introduced themselves. The brown-haired boy who had been riding the white pony was Jeremy, and his friend, who was darker-haired, was Benjamin. They asked me if I had gotten enough to eat, and I said yes.

I decided to eat a few grapes, so I turned back to the table. I broke off a small bunch, and as I began to eat the sweet yellow grapes, Vanessa appeared with a melon and a long, shiny knife. The size of the knife startled me, but she seemed to think nothing of it. The melon was smooth and whitish-yellow, almost the size of my head, and she cut it in two with one stroke of the knife. She set one half on the table, scraped the seeds of the other half into the cavity of the first one, and set the soft, luscious melon half in front of me.

I looked up at her and smiled. "Thank you."

"You're welcome, Daniel."

After such a full meal I fell asleep in the shade of the tent. I awoke in the late afternoon, feeling puffy and thirsty. I went to the stream, took a leisurely drink of water, and washed my face.

Back at the tent, Vanessa and Waneena sat on each side of the table with their elbows on the wood and their fingers sticking straight up. A third girl was stringing yarn back and forth between them. She had long brown hair and wore a loose, flowing dress like the other two. As she bent to wrap the yarn, I saw that just like the others, she didn't wear anything between her dress and her skin.

I turned my eyes away, and when I came back, she smiled and said, "You must be Daniel. I'm Lavonna."

I couldn't get over how nice these people were to me—especially such pretty girls, but the boys too. That evening I met more of them, boys with names like David and Michael and Christopher, and girls named Heather, Angelina, and Lenore. They set out another meal of bread and cheese and fruit and fresh roasted meat, and the conversation was happy up and down the table. After supper they gathered around a campfire, and they had me join them. One of the boys played an instrument like a large mandolin, and they sang songs about young love and the dew on the roses. I fell asleep by the campfire, and when I awoke in the middle of the night, I saw that the embers had burned down and someone had put a blanket over me.

* * * * *

I stayed in their village for two more days. After the newness wore off, I began to see things I hadn't noticed at first. For one, there didn't seem to be any men over the age of seventeen. There were women, and children, and even some old gummer white-haired crones, but only the young and the pretty and the handsome ate at the big table and gathered around the fire.

I also noticed that there were more girls than boys, which should have made for jealousy among the girls. But the opposite seemed to be the case. On the second night by the fire, when the singing was over, the boys began to pick the girls they wanted to go with them. I gathered that they did this every night, because the girls didn't resist. But the boys were stubborn and possessive. When there were four girls to choose from, two boys would argue over the same girl. Michael and David settled their argument after a while, but Benjamin and Jeremy argued for nearly an hour to see who went with Lavonna. At last she left with Benjamin, and I thought Jeremy was going to swing his staff at the other boy. Instead, he brought it down hard and broke it on one of the rocks by the fire. Then he threw the splintered pieces onto the coals, grabbed another girl's hand, and led her away.

The next day, everyone was calm and smiling again. Vanessa had taken to paying special attention to me, leaning over my shoulder to put more meat or bread close to my plate. She sat next to me and leaned toward me in conversation, and I could see the lovely slopes of her breasts. At the evening meal, she sliced a melon in half, scraped the seeds out like before, and set the clean half in front of me. She set the knife to her right on the other side of the half that had the mound of seeds in its center.

Beyond her, Jeremy sat across from Lavonna. At Lavonna's left, Benjamin sat hip-to-hip by her on the bench. Everything seemed polite as always until Benjamin's voice hit a sharp note. The table shook, and both Jeremy and Benjamin stood up and tried to hit each other across the table. Benjamin picked up a fork and stabbed Jeremy in the forearm, and that did it. Jeremy grabbed Benjamin by the tunic, dragged him across the table, and stood him up long enough to grab the melon knife and plunge it upwards into Benjamin's middle. The dark-haired boy let out a long, gasping groan and sank to the ground.

Jeremy flung the knife in the direction of the campfire and stomped away.

Lavonna buried her face in her hands and sobbed. "Oh, won't they ever quit?"

Vanessa leaned toward me and blocked my view of the boy who had just been stabbed. "Here, Daniel," she said. "Don't forget your melon."

I could tell she was talking to me, but she was looking across the table at Lavonna.

"I don't know," I said. "I'm not that hungry."

She leaned closer and pressed the peak of her dress against my arm. "I know you like it."

She sat close like that until somebody took the body away. A little while later, all the young people gathered at the fire again. The boy played his instrument, and they all sang songs about young love and dew on the roses.

In the first grey light of morning, I crawled out from under my blanket and walked away from the camp as quiet as I could. When I got to the bend in the stream, I ran like hell.

* * * * *

I found the hill where I had come out of the tunnel, but I

couldn't find the opening right away. I wandered up and down and back and forth across the hillside. Every so often I turned to study the layout of the stream and the trees and the green valley below, to see if I could get my bearings. Then I found the opening, with a fringe of brush growing around it. I stood for a few minutes to cool down and quit sweating. The sun was up and making its first quick climb. I took a long look at the valley, then turned and went into the passageway.

The light grew dimmer as I made my way in. At the point where the tunnel began to curve to the right, I saw a darker area to my left. As I felt out the wall, I discovered that another passage went off to the left. I had walked right past it on my way out, as I had been following the main tunnel toward the light.

I stood there and thought about my choices. I could follow the path back to the hole where I started, but there I would be with a rope that would do me no good. On the other hand, I could follow this unknown tunnel and see where it took me. If I came to a dead end, I could always find my way back to this spot and decide again.

It occurred to me that I could also try going out to the hillside and climbing up over the mountain. I hadn't thought of that earlier. I had just run in the way I had come out a few days before.

I decided it was worth a look. Now that I knew where I was going, I wasted no time getting back to the mouth of the tunnel. I crouched in the cover of the brush, and as I lifted my head to peek at the valley, I saw something that gave a jolt to my stomach. A brown-haired boy in a light-colored cape and tunic was riding a white pony along the treeline in the direction of my hillside.

I ducked back into the passageway and hurried along until I came to the side turnoff. *Here goes*, I thought, and I pushed into the darkness.

Within fifty yards I stumbled on a rock and fell. *Slow*, I told myself. No need to hurry. For all I knew, this trail could lead to a big yawning pit, and I could walk right off the edge into it.

I didn't, though. I took one cautious step after another, felt the hard earth walls with my hands, and moved through the body of the mountain. After a while I felt myself walking uphill. The route took a turn to the right and then the left, then continued sloping upward. I felt the walls on both sides to make sure I wasn't passing up any other side tunnels that I could wander into without knowing if I had to turn around and come back.

The thought of this whole mountain being a honeycomb of tunnels scared me, but I had to go on. I knew I couldn't get out the way I came in.

The path got steeper, and I had to lean forward. The tunnel made more turns, and then the darkness began to thin. I walked toward light until I came to a dead end where a shaft slanted upward about ten feet and opened to the blue sky.

This hole was a lot better than the one where the rope had fallen in on me, but the wall was still twice as high as I was. Furthermore, there were rocks all over the floor, rocks about the size of my head. I could imagine trying to pull myself up by my fingernails and having Jeremy throwing rocks down on me.

Then it occurred to me that the rocks might have a purpose. Somebody had been here before—probably whoever had found the gold coins at the bottom of the other hole—and that same somebody had most likely gone up the slanted wall. Not clawing with his fingernails, as I imagined myself doing, but climbing on a pyramid of rocks.

For all I knew, someone had spent countless hours gathering the rocks inside the bowels of the mountain. Of course someone could have dropped them down the hole as well. But I didn't waste much time on thinking about the last person. I started building my scaffold.

On my first try, I made it about halfway up until the rocks slipped out of place and I came sliding down, face forward. Rocks bounced off of me and settled on the floor.

I built up the wall again and gave it a second try. This time the rocks dislodged right away, and I jumped aside and scrambled out of the way of the slide.

I took a deep breath and started over. This time I made a deliberate effort to have the rocks make as much contact with the wall as possible. Then when I began to climb, I pressed my legs against the rocks rather than push straight down with my toes.

I inched my way up the wall until my face was rubbing against the dirt. After several minutes my chest was above the rocks, then my knees. I reached up for the ledge at the mouth of the hole, and I held myself still as I brought my other hand around. As I pulled, I also gave a push with my feet, and all the rocks went clacking and thudding to the floor of the hole. My cap fell away, and with dirt in my eyes, I pulled and pushed and squirmed my way up out of that pit.

When I made it onto solid ground, I rolled over onto my back and stared at the dull blue sky. The air was parched, and the sun was hot on my face. I had dirt scratches on my cheek and forehead, and my cap was down in the hole. I did not know where I was or which way I should go. Crumbly earth formations rose up on each side of me, and there was no plant life in sight. It was a place for spiders, lizards, and snakes.

As I lay there trying to shade my face and collect my strength, a sound came floating on the air. It was as soothing as a glass of cool water. I sat up and listened. It was the song of Pierre, bringing me back to the heat and misery of the desert. I was happy to be there, back in a world I understood.

I stood up and followed the sound, over the crumbles and clods and through a crevice in the wall of old dead mud. Below me on the desert floor, with his feet spread out and his head lowered, stood black Pierre. He was still tied to the bush, and he was braying to the world. *Wunh-hunh, wunh-hunh, wunh-hunh-hunh.*

Now I knew which way was north and which was west. I knew where Bonnet was and how to get there. I began to pick my way down through the rocks. When I had worked my way past the steepest part of the slope, I ran downhill until I came within a few yards of Pierre.

He had stopped bellowing when he saw me, and now he stared at me with his broad head and long ears rocking from side to side. I stopped short and remembered Cactus Pete.

185

The roan mare was gone, but when I looked toward the spot where we had uncovered the hole, I saw a dark shape lying on the ground.

More than I anything I wanted to high-tail it back to Bonnet, but I didn't think it would be right not to at least take a look at Cactus Pete and say I was sorry.

When I did, I saw the strangest thing. The blood on his shirt was still moist, as if he had been shot only a few minutes before, and neither the desert heat nor the scavengers had begun their work on him.

* * * * *

Back in town, I told the deputy marshal how to find the body. He and two other men went out and took care of things. I understood they buried Pete where he died. No one knew of any family for him, so the deputy told me I might as well keep Pierre for my troubles. What troubles they were, I did not tell anyone in detail, just that I had worked a few days without pay, had hidden in a hole when Pete got killed, and found my way back by myself.

So now I am doing odd jobs like before, sleeping on my cot in the livery stable, and trying to forget about the land on the other side of the mountain. Pierre wanders the streets of Bennet, where everyone knows him and shoos him away. In the evening he comes to the stable and calls. I feed him a few wisps of hay and wonder what goes on behind his heavy brow. At night I go to sleep knowing I have one friend in the world, and in the morning I wake to the song of Pierre.

Hap

A lone rider turned off the trail and onto the hard-packed dirt in front of the way station, the slow hoofbeats sounding hollow until they came to a stop. The dark horse snuffled, and when the man swung down from the saddle, the animal gave a rolling shake that rattled the stirrups. The horse was mid-sized and husky, with black mane, tail, and legs, while the shoulders and haunches shaded to a dark brown. His long winter hair bristled on his jaws and neck, and he had a worn, steady look to him as if he had been on the trail for a while. The bedroll and rifle scabbard appeared to be snugged on for the long ride as well.

The man wore a drab, low-brimmed hat, a double-caped grey wool coat that reached halfway from his waist to his knees, and a pair of charcoal-grey wool pants. Worn leather gloves, slick on the palm side and weathered across the knuckles, matched the scuffed boots and dull straps on his spurs. As the man loosened the cinch, he glanced in the direction of the board sign tacked to the wall on the right side of the station door. Stoneman's Bluff. The man turned and looked across the road, where a sandstone bluff rose out of the grass and sagebrush a quarter of a mile away. The late-morning sun cast pockets of shadow where the elements had chiseled features on the face of the bluff.

The door of the station opened with a scraping sound, and a man's voice sang out.

"Hullo, there. Anything we can do for ya?"

The traveler turned toward the doorway. "What's the chance of gettin' a bite to eat?"

"Pretty good. Tie up your horse and come on in."

The interior was dim as well as chilly. The station-keeper, wearing a dark knitted cap and a canvas coat, bustled about as he threw a couple of chunks of firewood into the cast-iron stove. He turned to his guest, showing a pair of watery blue eyes and a week's worth of grey stubble.

"I hope bacon and spuds agree with you, 'cause that's what I've got."

"Then that's what I like to eat."

"Good." As the older man went about slicing a few withered potatoes, he kept up a string of chatter. Been cold, lots of wind, not much snow. Stage used to come through but doesn't any more. More ranches than there used to be, though, and would-be dirt-farmers that come out with not much more than the shirt on their back. Nesters. Eat everyone else's beef, come and beg bacon grease. Cow-punchers are a different story. A lot of them boys go back home and feed hogs through the winter. Coal, now, there's work in that, and in the winter time, too.

He set the skillet on the stove top, cut half a dozen slices from a slab of bacon, and laid them in. Turning to look at his patron, he said, "You a puncher, too?"

"Sometimes."

"Well, don't mind me. It's just somethin' to talk about."

"Sure."

The old man poked at the strips of bacon with his knife. "Didn't notice which way you came in from."

"Travelin' north."

"That's what I thought. Goin' to the Black Hills?"

"Don't know. Depends on where my trail takes me."

"It's been an open winter, and travel's not too bad. Fella the other day said he come down from Miles City, on his way to Denver. Now that's a long ride, this time of year."

"I'd say."

"You wanna go east, now that's different. You can take a train a good part of the way. You like salt?"

"A little bit."

"These spuds can use it." He pointed with his knife at the raw slices on the cutting board. Then he laid the knife down and said, "I'd better get some coffee going."

By the time he put the coffee pot on the stove top, the bacon was sputtering. He flipped the pieces, let them cook for a minute more, and lifted them out onto a tin plate. Then he slid the potato slices into the skillet. "This'll stick to your ribs." After a pause he added, "You say you're not goin' to Deadwood, then."

"It's not my intention."

"Just as good. There's men there that'll cut your throat for the price of a bottle of whiskey."

"If you let 'em." Silence hung until the man in grey spoke again. "Been a bit of traffic, then?"

"Some, but you don't see 'em all."

"I imagine."

"There's one fella they think came through here, but they're not sure."

"Oh."

With his thumb and two fingers, the old man lifted a pinch of salt out of a little wooden box and scattered the grains across the top of the cooking potatoes. "Bad sort, name of Ace Perkins. They say he stopped at a ranch house down by Shawnee, where a man and his wife were livin' by themselves. This Perkins, as the story goes, tied the husband up, cut off all the woman's hair, and then had his way with her, with the man havin' to sit there and not be able to do anythin' about it. Then he shoots the man, burns down their house, and makes off with the woman. Next day he stops at a homesteader's place, kills him, takes the woman into that cabin and does who-knows-what, and burns all her clothes. Leaves her there wrapped in a blanket, with snow on the ground outside, and goes on his way. They're lookin' for him."

"The woman lived through it, then."

"Not in very good shape, but she was able to tell what happened and describe him. That's how they know it's Perkins."

"Sounds like a bad one. What's he look like, anyway?"

"They say he's about average height, kind of stocky. Got a wall-eye, and no pointer finger on his right hand, though I've heard you wouldn't know it from the way he handles a gun."

"So everyone's on the lookout for him."

"Like I said, the word's out. And there's a reward." The old man's glance took in the guest, who sat with his coat unbuttoned and his six-gun in view. The proprietor narrowed his eyes. "You're not after him, are you?"

The man in grey shook his head. "No."

"Too bad. The more the better, for that son of a bitch." The eyebrows went up. "But you're lookin' for someone, huh?"

The traveler didn't answer.

"You're not sayin'. Well, that's all right, too. Like I said, it's all just a way of makin' conversation while the grub cooks." The old man put his hands out to take in the heat of the stove. "Warmin' up in here all right. By the way, my name's Dean. Harry Dean."

"Mine's Cooper."

"Good to meet you, Cooper. Here, why don't you eat the bacon before it gets cold, and I'll have these spuds ready in a few minutes."

The man in grey opened a jack knife and tipped it to one side as the host set the plate on the table.

* * * * *

The features on Stoneman's Bluff had darkened when the traveler came out of the road house. He put a bundle in the near saddlebag, untied the horse, and led him out a few steps. The station man called from the doorway.

"You come back this way, stop in."

The grey hat brim lifted, and the man looked across his saddle as he snugged the cinch. "I'll do that."

* * * * *

By late afternoon the sky had gone overcast and the sunlight had weakened. The dark horse kept a steady pace as the trail ran parallel to a dry watercourse. Up ahead on the right, a fire blazed in front of a canvas-topped wagon. Farther back from the camp site, two sorrel horses grazed on picket ropes. A bearded man crouched by the fire, while another stood at the tailgate of the wagon.

The man in grey reined his horse about a hundred feet out from the wagon and called, "Hello the camp."

The man by the fire stood up and said, "Come on in."

The rider swung down and led the horse into the camp as the man from the back of the wagon came into view. Both he and his partner looked over the newcomer's outfit.

"Long trail," said the man by the fire, who was the shorter of the two.

"Sure is. You're the first two fellas I've seen since I left Stoneman's Bluff."

"You stop there?"

"That I did. Had a hot meal with the old man who runs the place."

"He likes company."

The traveler smiled. "Seems to."

The taller man, who had a knife in his hand, spoke up. "You're probably about ready to eat again."

"The thought would occur."

"Well, you're welcome to eat with us. We've got plenty. I'm just now cuttin' it up."

"Oh, I don't know . . . ."

"We've got plenty," the man said again. "We're hunters. No fine wines or tropical fruit, but you won't find us livin' on cold flapjacks, either. We got good deer meat."

"I'd hate to be the kind to turn it down."

As the steaks sizzled in the skillet, the two men gave an account of themselves. The taller one was named White, and his partner was O'Neill. They'd been trapping and hunting all winter and had just sold their pelts and hides. O'Neill made a point of saying they had put the money in the bank. Now they were meat hunting, and picking up a few more hides, until the ranch work started.

White stabbed a piece of meat and flipped it over. "How 'bout yourself?"

"Lookin' for work."

"What kind?"

"Ranch work, if I can get it."

O'Neill spoke up. "It's a little early for that. About the only work we've seen, and not up close, is out-of-the-way work. Cinch-ring artists, runnin'-iron men. We stay away from them."

"That's the best."

"You bet. And you know how the big outfits are. If they do it, it's all fair. But if someone else does, he's a rustler."

"Has there been a little bit of it, then?"

"It's hard to say. The way they set up a howl, you'd think there was legions out there. And they brought in a stock detective."

The man in grey lifted his head. "Is that right?"

White took his turn at speaking. "Fella by the name of Stook Wilson."

"Do you know him?" O'Neill asked.

"I think I might have heard the name."

"He's not hard to pick out," O'Neill went on. "He rides a dark horse, darker'n yours, and he dresses in black. Wears a dark overcoat and carries a black slicker. They say it's for night work, and I believe it. He works for three or four of the big outfits, moves around from one to another. Drops in on people's camps at any time of the day or night."

"Around here?"

"He works this whole country from the Cheyenne River down to the Niobrara."

"How long has he been here?"

O'Neill looked at White. "What, about three months?"

"Something like that. Long enough to pick off a few."

"No one does anything?"

O'Neill shook his head. "No proof. A man steps out of his cabin door in the morning, and that's it. Wilson disappears for a little while, someone sees him up in Deadwood on a three-day drunk. They say he passes out in a whore's room, where he gets his money's worth about half the time."

"Is he there now?"

"No, he's been back for a couple of weeks. They've seen him around in the past few days."

"Around here?"

O'Neill motioned with his head. "Over west and a little north of here. Near Corrigan Dome."

"What's that like?"

"Oh, kinda ugly country. Oil seeps, alkali flats. Right by the Dome there's a spring, where sulfur-smellin' water comes out all year round. Warm water. I wouldn't drink it, but it's good for any other purposes—you know, clean up, wash clothes. Anyway, there's a cabin at that spot, and they say Wilson hangs out there when he's in between jobs."

"West of here, you say, and a little north."

O'Neill gave a close glance. "Are you lookin' for someone?"

"I'm lookin' for work. But if there's someone like that out there, I don't mind knowin' where he is. Stay out of his way and go about my own business."

White spoke again. "Be glad to help if we could. What's your name, anyway?"

"Cooper. Jim Cooper."

"It'll be a while till anyone's puttin' on more men, but we'll remember your name."

"Appreciate it. Never know when it might help."

"You bet," said White. "Meanwhile, don't be shy. You can roll your bed out here tonight, have some good hot coffee before you hit the trail in the mornin'."

"That's mighty good of you boys. I'll remember you for it."

* * * * *

The flat country sloping away from Corrigan Dome looked bleak in the pale light of an overcast afternoon. Outside the cabin, two horses were picketed on sparse grass. A wisp of smoke rose from the stovepipe, and a small cloud of mist showed where the warm water came out of the spring.

The man in grey pushed himself up onto his feet and side-stepped down the hill to his horse. He put the field glasses in the saddle bag, checked to see that his six-gun was in place, and swung aboard.

He rode half a mile across the flat, slow hoofbeats thudding as he approached the cabin. When he had come within thirty yards, he stopped and called out a greeting.

The cabin door opened, and a dark, lean figure in a tall-crowned hat appeared, rifle in hand. "What do you want?" he called.

"Wonderin' if I could put up for the night. I think I lost my road."

"Where is it that you think you're goin'?"

"They said there was a way to get to the Powder River country."

"There's more than one way, but you're a good twenty miles from the closest one."

The traveler let out a long sigh. "I've been ridin' since sunup. I could camp outside if it's all right with you."

"Naw, hell." The man in the doorway turned and said something, then looked outward again. "Come on in."

The two horses on picket, one dark and one sorrel, watched as the man rode a little further, then dismounted and led the saddled horse.

"There's a lean-to in back," said the man with the rifle, not so loud now. "You can leave your gear there and put your horse out near the others."

"Good enough."

Inside the lean-to, a small pile of firewood, none of the pieces bigger around than a man's wrist, sat by the back door. Against the far wall, one saddle sat on a rack while another rested off-center on a battered box. The man in grey laid his saddle and all its gear on the floor against the side wall. Then he set the horse out to graze with the other two on the meager grass.

He stood still for a long moment. The sun was slipping in the west now, and the evening chill was setting in. The sulfur smell from the hot spring hung in the air, and the world was quiet except for the shifting of horse hooves.

The front door of the cabin was ajar, so he knocked on the door frame and pushed the door open. Two men sat at a table in the middle of the room. The man in the tall black hat was facing the entry, while the other, not so lean and not so tense, sat at a right angle from him and also watched the door. To the right of the table, a small sheet-iron stove showed a glow through the half-open hatch.

"Come on in," said the man in the black hat. "Pull up a chair."

The second man, who wore a brown hat and leather vest, pointed at a cane-bottom chair next to the stove. A woolen undershirt was draped across the back, as if it had been set out to dry. "Just gimme the shirt," he said.

The man in grey picked up the chair, tilted it to the stocky man who had just spoken, and held the pose for a few seconds. As the other man took the shirt, his wall-eye came into view. He laid the garment in his lap and turned back to the table, where a whiskey bottle stood between two glasses.

The newcomer took a seat about three feet from the table and perpendicular to it, so that his back was not to the door either.

"What's yer name?" asked the man with the wall-eye.

"Bell. Tom Bell."

"Huh. Seems I've heard that before."

"It's a common name. And yours?"

"Just call me Ace."

"Pleased to." He turned to the man in the black hat. "And yourself?"

"Wilson." The man had green eyes, the shade of bottle glass, and his hair was the color of autumn corn stalks. "Where you comin' from?"

"I come in from the east, by way of Harrison."

"What news along the way?"

"Don't know. I didn't talk to anyone very much. Just enough to get off on the wrong trail, I guess."

"You sleep out?"

"Last night I camped with a couple of hunters, but I didn't talk to them very much. My piles were botherin' me, and I turned in early." He paused. "At least I ate good."

Ace shifted in his chair. "We were just startin' to think about grub ourselves. That time of day."

"I'll tell you what. I bought a hunk of bacon a couple of days ago, and I'd be glad to contribute it."

"That would be all right." Ace wrapped three fingers around his whiskey glass, just as natural as if he had all four.

Wilson and Ace paid no attention as the visitor got up and went to the back door. In the dusk of the lean-to he rummaged for the piece of bacon. Before straightening up, he laid his hand on the stock of the rifle, gave the gun a tug, and eased it back into the scabbard.

Both men's eyes were on him as he stepped inside. He set the bundle on the table and unwrapped the coarse paper. Then he opened his jack knife and began cutting slices.

"Guess I'll chunk up the fire," said Ace. He let out a long breath through his nose, then turned toward the stove. As he did, his holster and pistol rode up into view.

Wilson spoke in a sharp tone. "No news, then, huh?"

"Didn't ask for any."

"You say you came in from Harrison?"

"Through there."

"And what have you got in mind for the Powder River country?"

"Lookin' for work."

"It's a little early for that. Anyone who's out on the range right now is likely to be up to no good. These outfits won't even bring in their horses for another three or four weeks."

The newcomer did not answer.

Ace settled into his earlier pose with his fingers curled around his whiskey glass. "We've got time for at least one more snow before the range work starts up."

"Maybe," said Wilson, who then made a sucking sound, as if he was cleaning out a molar with his tongue.

Ace took a sip of whiskey. "I know a couple outfits, they go to Cheyenne and hire a full crew of men, and then walk 'em all the way back to this country. Like prisoners. Then they bring in the horses, and each man gentles his own string."

Wilson sniffed. "Not everyone does it the same. These outfits that've been around for a while, they have a lot of the same men come back every year."

The man in grey laid half a dozen strips of bacon in a crusty skillet, then crossed in back of Ace to put the pan on the stove. Wilson's eyes followed him as he returned to the table and resumed slicing.

"Thing is," continued Ace, "a lot of these fellas are no better'n hoboes. Got nothin' more'n the clothes they're wearin'. Takes the first month for 'em to get rid of the shakes."

"Some are that way," said Wilson, who was now working his left side with a toothpick. "Not all."

"I didn't say all. I just said 'a lot.' They don't have their own saddle, and some of 'em have to learn to ride a horse. They get a real edgi-cation."

"You seem to know a great deal." Wilson hiked his right foot up onto the other knee and sat up straight. His boots were black, scuffed on the toes from going in and out of stirrups, and he wasn't wearing spurs. Quiet.

Ace tipped his head up and smiled. "This ain't my first time out in the country."

The man in grey folded his knife and put it away. He passed in back of Ace, crossed to the other side of the stove, took out his knife and opened it, and began poking the bacon slices. The skillet had heated enough that the fat was starting to melt.

Wilson's voice came up again. "What outfits do you know of, over in the Powder River country?"

The man at the stove shrugged. "None yet."

"There's the Hoe outfit," said Ace. "They're a big one. And the Six Pines. I've heard of it."

"There's a bunch," said Wilson, clipping the last word. "I was just askin' if he knows of any." Then, raising his chin and lightening his tone, he said, "Damn, I've forgotten your name already. What did you say it was?"

"Tom Bell."

"Sure. That's right."

"I'm certain I've heard that name," said Ace. "Seems to me it was someone who got into a jackpot."

"I don't doubt it," said the man at the skillet. "Like I said before, it's a common name."

Wilson leveled his gaze now, the pale green eyes looking like a cat's. "Have you got any heel-flies after you, Bell?"

"Not that I know of. I haven't done anything."

Ace gave a coarse, short laugh. "Nobody ever does." After a couple of seconds of silence he went on, as if to rectify what he just said. "Like that back-shootin' Frank Canton. Now there's someone to know in the Powder River country."

Wilson's voice came up sharp again. "Why do you call him that?"

Ace shrugged. "Why not? That's what he is."

Wilson's face drew hard and tight. "People shouldn't say things they don't have proof of."

"People are afraid to talk. That's why they haven't been able to prove anything against him."

"I'll tell you this," said Wilson, his voice tense. "People are afraid to say it to his face, that's what. But they say it behind his back."

"Well, there's people right there in the Powder River country that know where he came from, what his name was then, and why he left."

"Talk's cheap. That's why there's so much of it."

Silence took over for a little while. The bacon fat sputtered, and the man with the knife flipped the pieces.

"Is there anything else to go along with this?" he asked.

"There's some biscuits," said Ace. "They're a day old, but they're all right." He pointed with his three fingers toward the back wall, where a heap of kitchen objects sat on a wooden crate. "Over there in a tin plate, covered with that cloth."

The man in grey fetched the biscuits and two additional tin plates. He set the cloth on the table and the biscuits on top of it, then laid out the three plates. Using a glove to hold the skillet handle, he lifted the fried bacon pieces with his knife and set them three in one plate and three in another.

"Go ahead," he said. "I'll eat from the second batch." He put the skillet on the stove and laid the remaining six slices in the hot grease. The pan crackled.

Ace pushed a plate toward Wilson and drew the other to himself. Then he reached for two biscuits. "Good grub," he said. "Never pass up a hot meal, for you never know when the next one'll be." He lifted a piece of bacon with his right hand, the big finger serving as first finger, and bit off a chunk. "Damn good," he said, smacking his lips.

The white strips were swimming in grease, and a thin black smoke rose from the pan.

Came the smacking sound again as Ace took another bite. His finger and thumb were greasy, and the top of his chin had taken on a shine as well. "Three things to enjoy in this life, whenever you can. There's good grub, good drink, and good snatch. Don't you think so, Tom?"

"I suppose." The man who called himself Tom Bell flipped a slice of bacon.

"'Course, you know what they say. It's all good, just some of it's better. Speakin' of snatch, of course."

Wilson unbuttoned his coat and scooted his chair up to the table, showing no hurry to start eating.

Ace waved a stub of bacon in the air as he held forth. "Thing is, you can make it better. Last one I had, she was slobberin' and beggin'. Now that's when it's good, when you've got her broken like a whipped dog."

Wilson tilted his head and gave a narrow, sideways glance. "You know, you've got a low-class way about you."

"Call it that if you want." Ace took a drink of whiskey. "But maybe you don't know how much the old devil rises up in a man and makes him throb till he thinks he's gonna split."

"You talk too much."

"Aw, hell," he said, with a backward wave of his free hand. "Maybe all you've ever done is pay for it. But if you just take it, get that woman broken, the whole pleasure runs a lot deeper."

"Ah, shut up."

"No, I mean it. When you get 'em whipped so—"

His words were cut off by a blast of gunfire, piercing loud in the close space of the cabin. Ace fell back, the chair skidding out from under him as he glanced off the corner of the stove and sprawled on the floor with the woolen undershirt still in his lap.

The man in grey had jumped back and now reached for the skillet to get it centered on the stove again. He turned to look at Wilson, who had turned in his chair and still had his gun pointed at the man on the floor.

"No need to get shook up," said the gunman. "There's a reward for this fella, so he was gonna get it sooner or later. Just came sooner, from not knowin' when to shut up." Wilson had his eyebrows lifted as he surveyed the dead man. "Let's get that gun out of his holster—no, I'll do it. Just stand by for a minute." He stood up from his chair, slipped his dark-handled six-gun into his holster, and bent forward to reach for the ivory grip on Ace Perkins's pistol.

In that instant, with a backhand swing of his left hand, the man at the stove swung the skillet and flung the hot grease and bacon pieces in Wilson's face. As the gunman rose, took a staggering step backward, and clawed for his gun, the man in grey drew his own pistol and shot Wilson twice in the chest.

The tall-crowned black hat went flying, and the man's arms flailed as he spilled over backwards.

With his pistol still drawn, the man in grey walked around the other side of the table, avoiding the knocked-over chairs and sprawled bodies. He stood above Wilson, whose fresh-blistered face, framed by the shock of hair the color of corn stalks, was motionless. His thin lips pressed together with a seam of blood.

"Stook Wilson," said the man holding the gun. "I don't know if you can hear this, but it does me good to say it. My name isn't what I said it was. It's actually Hapgood. Maybe that name rings a bell with you."

* * * * *

The man in the double-caped coat stood in silhouette, holding the reins of his saddled horse as the flames from the cabin lit up the night. When the first section of the roof fell in, he moved to each of the other two horses, which had pulled back to the ends of their pickets, and he untied them. Their hoof-beats died away as they headed for the open range. A soft thud sounded from the cabin as another rafter fell in, sending a shower of sparks upward. The man turned his horse so that the saddle leather shone in the firelight. He put his foot in the stirrup, swung aboard, and rode away.

* * * * *

Stoneman's Bluff frowned in the shadows of early afternoon

as the man in grey turned off the trail and rode up to the hitching rail in front of the way station.

Old Harry Dean appeared in the doorway, again in his dark knitted cap and canvas coat. "Oh, it's you," he called out.

"It sure is." The rider swung down and tied his horse.

"What did you find out?"

"Not much. It's too early to get work."

"That's all you were lookin' for, huh?"

"Look for more, you look for trouble."

"Isn't that the truth? But I was hopin' you were lookin' for Ace Perkins. Too bad you didn't come back with him tied across a saddle." The old man shook his head. "Someone ought to take him down, and there's a good reward for the man that does it."

"Well, maybe so, but not me. I wouldn't kill for money, and I'm glad I'm not in that line of work."

"You gotta be good at it." The old man doubled his fist and gave it a quick shake at chest height, and his watery blue eyes flashed.

"Yeah, and even men who think they're good at it get tripped up. Maybe some of 'em live to an old age and die in their bed, but I'd guess even they have to be lookin' over their shoulder. As for the others, they might do well to remember that the more men they kill, the better the chance is that one of 'em's got a brother or some other kin that might come callin' some day. Nah, I'm glad I'm not in the business."

"Can't argue with you on that." The old man motioned with his head. "I've got some coffee goin'. Come on in and chin for a little while, Cooper."

"I guess I can. By the way, you can just call me Hap."

Strangers in Silverthorne

I was sweeping the front porch of the boarding house at the end of a dusty summer day when I saw a man come in from the east. He was riding a dark horse and leading a sorrel with canvas packs. I was used to strangers in Silverthorne, usually passing through on their way to somewhere else, so I didn't stand and stare like some people might.

When I looked up from my work again, I saw that he had come to a stop a few yards away. He wore a dust-colored hat and the drab clothes of a traveler. His saddle horse was dark brown with a black mane and tail.

"Do you work here?" the man asked.

"Sometimes. I work in one place and another as they need me."

"It's good to see boys who work, don't you think?"

"I guess."

He tossed the lead rope over the hitching rail, then swung down and wrapped his reins. He ducked under the dark horse's neck and tied the packhorse with a release knot. Everything was light and easy with him, and he came out from between the horses with his hat tipped to one side.

"Could you tell me where to find Mr. Dodd?"

I pointed across the street, to the left of where Mudrick the barber stood in his doorway. "Two doors down from the barber shop."

"Thanks," he said. "What's your name?"

"Alex."

"Mine's Fergus. Here."

He flipped a coin up and across the sidewalk. It flashed in the sunlight, and I could tell it was a quarter before I caught it.

"Thanks. What's it for?"

"Keepin' an eye on my horses."

"Nobody bothers anything in this town."

He smiled. "I wouldn't expect anyone to." Then he turned and angled across the street. Mudrick the barber raised his chin and watched the newcomer walk by.

About twenty minutes later, Fergus came back the same way. He was cheerful as he spoke to me from the foot of the steps. "How old are you, Alex?"

"Sixteen."

"Have you got time to do a little work for me?"

"Right now?"

"Well, yes. But after today as well. You see, I just rented Mr. Dodd's empty building."

"Which one?" Mr. Dodd had bought up several buildings on the main street. When someone went broke, Mr. Dodd bought the property cheap.

"The one that used to be a notions store. Straight across from his office."

"I see."

"If you've got a little while, I need to move some things in there. But if you're too busy—"

"Oh, no. I can help. I was just waiting for you to come back."

I went down the steps and stood as he untied the horses. He handed me the lead rope to the packhorse, and I walked in the street next to him as he led the saddle horse. We tied up at the rail in front of the empty store.

"Seems like a nice town," he said.

"Not much happens."

He ran his fingers under the cinch on the dark horse. "What do your folks do?"

"I don't have any. I live in a room in the back of Mrs. Colby's boarding house."

"Nothing wrong with that. Workin' for a living, I mean. Sorry you don't have any family."

"I'm used to it." I glanced over my shoulder at the packhorse. "What kind of store are you opening?"

"An honest little tobacco shop, Alex. A place where men can come and read the newspaper, maybe play a game of cards." He smiled at me. "What do you think of that?"

I shrugged. "It's all right, I guess."

"A boy I knew when he was growin' up, he lived with his grandma. She thought cards were evil. Called 'em the 'euchre deck.' What do you think of 'em?"

I thought it was remarkable that grown men could spend hours on end making small talk, laying down cards, and not knowing whether it was night or day outside. I said, "I think it's the people, not the cards. And even then, I haven't seen much evil. Mostly, cards just seem like a way to spend a lot of time."

"I think that's it. If a man's got evil in him, cards might bring it out. So can liquor, or any of a variety of things." He held up a key. "Well, let's go in."

The store was about twenty-five feet wide and forty feet deep, not very big. To the left of the doorway, a set of stairs led up to a loft where a window up on the front wall let in sunlight. An office area sat perched there, with a half-wall on the two interior sides, and a post that held up the platform and reached to the ceiling. Attached to the post was a pulley with a cord that ran down to a matching pulley at the sales counter. A cashbox was bolted to the counter top.

Fergus ran his fingers across the dark-stained wood. "Pretty dusty. We'll need to clean up. But we'll get our stuff in here first." He motioned with his head. "There's a room in back where I'll stay."

* * * * *

Fergus was in the loft when I showed up the next morning. The front door latch was on the left side, so when I opened the door and the bell rang, I saw him as he turned away from the window.

"Hello," he said. "Come on in." He took light steps as he came down the stairs.

We went to work, sweeping and dusting. Fergus used a worn broom to knock down cobwebs, and he didn't seem to be afraid of getting dirty. When we had the place presentable, I helped him unpack his tobacco tins, cigar boxes, sacks of Bull Durham, and sealed pouches of chewing tobacco.

"Do you use any of this stuff?" he asked.

"Not yet."

"Just as well. Neither do I. Not that I'm bein' all that superior by resistin' temptation. I just never got the habit, which is good, because I won't be smokin' up all my profits."

He rummaged in the pack and brought out a metal tube, the kind that people carry maps in. He uncapped it and slid out a scroll, which consisted of two lithograph posters. One had a picture of a little boy sitting in a washtub with his knees folded up as a lady in a high-necked dress sat on a stool and read from a book. The second poster looked like the cover of a dime novel, as it had a frontiersman on a rearing horse. He was aiming a rifle at a standing bear.

I held the posters as Fergus tacked them to the wall across the room from the counter. "What now?" I asked.

"We wait for business." He raised his eyebrows. "If you've got other work to do, you can go."

When I came back in the afternoon, Fergus was seated alone at a card table, which had appeared along with six chairs. He was cleaned up now, with his dark hair combed and his full mustache looking neat against his freshly shaven face. He was wearing a white shirt, a dark brown vest, and a pair of charcoal-colored pants.

"Good to see you," he said. "I'm so busy I can't leave the store." He laid a quarter on the table and pushed it toward me. "Why don't you go get us two root beers and about two pounds of peanuts?"

When I returned with the order, he told me to sit down and help myself to the peanuts. "As soon as I know my way around a little better, I'll keep a big sack of these on hand. Card players eat peanuts."

So did the other loafers I'd seen, but I didn't say anything. I nodded and took a drink from my root beer.

"Where do you get your hair cut?" he asked.

"Mrs. Colby cuts it for me."

He looked me over. "What would you think of goin' to the barber across the street? I'll pay for it."

"I don't know."

"Here's the deal. I want to see what kind of a haircut he gives before I find out for myself. Mrs. Colby wouldn't mind, not when you tell her I plan to order all my sandwiches from her."

"When will you do that?"

"As soon as I start having card games."

* * * * *

Mudrick the barber was as disagreeable up close as he was at a distance. He snugged the apron around my neck and then tipped the chair back as if he was going to give me a shave. But he didn't, of course. He just looked me over, standing in back of my head and peering down. Being a barber, he was also the undertaker, and his wife, who had a seamstress shop next door, helped him fit out corpses for burial. As he gazed at me now, with his hawk-like features and rough complexion upside-down, I imagined being a corpse that could look up and see him. Then in the silence I noticed something odd. His dark hair seemed to be much lighter at the roots.

His voice startled me. "Just a regular trim, eh?"

"That's right."

He jacked the chair up straight, turned it a few degrees, and stopped it with a firm grip. "You're the boy that works for Mrs. Colby, aren't you?"

"Yes, I am."

"Looks like you do jobs for this new fella, too."

From the way he said "fella," I could tell he didn't care for the new businessman in town. "A little," I said.

"What's his name?"

"Fergus."

"Is he Irish?"

"I don't know."

"Where's he come from?"

"I don't know that either."

"I heard he wants to put in gambling."

"I believe he has a card table."

Mudrick breathed out through his nose. "As if two saloons wasn't enough."

He cut my hair in less than five minutes, and when I gave him the quarter he gave me a dime in change.

"Is that all it costs?" I asked.

"For kids." He said it with as little affection as he had said "fella" earlier.

When I gave Fergus his change and explained the price, he laughed. "He's a regular citizen, isn't he? I'm sure he makes it up on dead people. That's his wife next door, eh?"

I pictured the woman, brown-haired and pale. "Yeah."

"And who else do they have livin' there?"

"I guess it's the girl who helps Mrs. Mudrick with her sewing."

"And she's got two little girls of her own."

I recalled the little girls, sun-heads like their mother. None of the three came out any more often than Mrs. Mudrick did, and I wondered how Fergus knew so much about them already. "That's right," I said. "They keep to themselves."

Fergus shrugged. "Some people are like that. The good barber himself doesn't seem very friendly."

"He hasn't ever struck me that way."

"Was this the first time you saw him up close?"

"Yes, it was."

"How old would you say he is?"

"I don't know. Maybe fifty. It's hard to tell. I don't have much experience at that, and besides, it looks like he dyes his hair."

"That doesn't surprise me." With a quick voice he added, "Bein' a barber, I imagine he does a neater job of it than the Comanches do."

I frowned. "How do they do it?"

"Oh, when they capture white people and keep 'em, which would be women or kids, they use grease and horse manure. On the light-haired ones, of course." Fergus tipped his head. "It's what I heard. Never tried it myself."

* * * * *

Within a week, Fergus was having card games. They began in the late afternoon and sometimes lasted all night as the chips migrated from one side of the table to another. Mrs. Colby said she didn't want me coming in at all hours, so I ran errands for Fergus from about six in the evening until ten at night. Sometimes he sat in on the game, and sometimes he stood by and kept an eye on it. I fetched beer from the saloons and went to the boarding house for sandwiches. In between times, as well as earlier in the day, I swept and cleaned up.

One evening as I was on my way to work at the tobacco shop, I saw a lady get off the stage. She was wearing a close-fitting cloth hat and a linen duster, but I could tell she was young and pretty. I lingered on the sidewalk and heard her tell the coachman to leave her trunk at the boarding house and she would walk there to get some exercise.

That night I heard from Mrs. Colby that the lady's name was Miss Morrie and she was going to open a book shop next door where old Kessler the shoemaker used to be.

"These little businesses have never done anything but die in this town," said Mrs. Colby. "I don't know how she can make it with a book shop, but she's very nice, and I don't want to say anything discouraging."

It occurred to me that Kessler's business died because he did, and Fergus' business was doing well, but I knew a great many others had failed. I hoped the best for Miss Morrie.

The next day I presented myself in the doorway of her shop. She was taking books out of a pasteboard box, and she paused with a book in her hands as she turned to me. She was wearing a woman's business suit—a grey jacket and skirt with a white blouse. She had blue eyes and brown hair, and her face seemed even prettier than the day before. I figured her for about ten years older than I was, and to use a phrase, I was smitten.

"Good day," she said as she laid the book on the counter. "How may I help you?"

I stepped inside. "My name's Alex. I stay at Mrs. Colby's, and I do work for her as well as others around town." I smiled as I raised my head. "I'm at your service."

Her face softened with a smile. "How nice of you. I'm sure I'll need something before long, but as you can see, I'm not set up yet. And I have more things on the way."

"Mrs. Colby says you're to have a book shop."

"That's my idea."

"What kind of books?"

"Do you like to read?"

"Oh, I've read some."

"Well, I plan to have Bibles and prayer books, volumes by the schoolroom poets, wholesome fiction, biography, Grant's memoirs of course, and other things as people ask for them. Lectures, perhaps, and humor. Bill Nye, for example. What was the last book you read?"

I felt myself blush. "*Frank at Don Carlos' Rancho*."

"Oh, yes. Harry Castlemon. I might order some of his."

"I can read more serious things. I've read *The Oregon Trail* and *Two Years Before the Mast*."

"That's good."

I hesitated. "I hope you do well. I don't know how many people would buy books in Silverthorne, though."

She smiled again in her lovely way. "Oh, I plan to have a few other things as well. Women's accessories, like bonnets, shawls, and gloves."

I didn't know what to say next, so after a few seconds of silence I said, "Well, I guess I should move along and let you get settled in."

"I'm glad you stopped, Alex. Come any time."

"Thank you, Miss—Morrie, isn't it?"

"That's right. Evelyn Morrie." She gave me her hand.

I was almost afraid to touch her. She was like a goddess. I pressed my fingers against hers, then let go and backed away. "Good-bye," I said.

"Good-bye."

I stepped out into the sunlight, and my head was in a swirl. As I collected myself, I thought I should let Fergus know there was a new woman in town.

He barely looked up from his ledger when I told him. "That's all I need," he said. "Someone to try to shut my business down."

"Oh, you haven't seen her yet."

Without looking up he said, "Don't be so sure."

* * * * *

I was sweeping up the last of the peanut shells after a card game that had run late the night before. Fergus was up in the crow's nest where he spent quite a bit of his time during the day.

"Alex."

"Yes."

"Come over here to the stairs. I don't want to holler."

I leaned my broom against the table, crossed the room, and went up the stairway a few steps. "Yes, sir?"

"I say, um, you know Miss Morrie, don't you?"

"Well, yes, I do."

"And you know how to keep something under your hat?"

"Of course."

"Look here." He bore down on me with his dark eyes. "I'd like you to deliver a note for me. Don't carry it where anyone will see it, and don't give it to her if anyone else is around. Top secret, you know what I mean?"

"I do."

"And if she wants to send a note back, give her time to write it. Then don't come straight back here. Now that I think of it, don't go straight there, either. Mix things up, you know."

"Very well." I took the envelope and tucked it inside my shirt. I went out the door, turned left, crossed the street, went around the back of the buildings, came out by the livery stable, crossed over to the boarding house, then sauntered down the sidewalk and stepped into Evelyn Morrie's shop.

She stood up behind the counter. She was wearing the same outfit as before, and she looked clean and prim. "Well, hello, Alex. How are you today?"

"Just fine, Miss Morrie."

She gave me a close look. "Is there something . . . wrong?"

"No, not at all." I lowered my voice. "I have a message for you."

"Oh." She didn't seem surprised.

I reached inside my shirt and found the envelope where it was sticking to my damp skin. I stepped close and handed it to her.

"Thank you." She took it and sat down on the wooden stool behind the counter. With a serious expression on her face she opened the envelope and read the letter.

"I'm to wait for an answer if you want to write one."

"I think I will."

No one came into the shop as I loitered with a copy of *Little Women* in my hands. After several minutes I heard the rustle of paper and then Evelyn Morrie's voice.

"Here it is. Don't lose it, by all means."

"Safe and sound." I tucked it in where the other one had been.

"Thank you, Alex. You're a dear."

"Any time."

I put on a casual air and walked out of her shop. I turned right, went past the boarding house, turned at the corner, and came back through the alley. On a hunch I tried the back door of Fergus' building, but it was locked. Without thinking I tried it a second time, and I heard the latch turn as I felt the doorknob pulled from my hand. Fergus stood in the doorway pointing a blue-black revolver at me.

"Oh, it's you."

I frowned at the gun. "Sorry."

"Come on in," he said as he lowered the gun and stepped aside. "I just don't like surprises."

* * * * *

For the next few days I carried messages as much as I went for beer and sandwiches. On the part of both Fergus and Eve-lyn, as I now thought of her, there seemed to be some kind of an urgency, a desire to not lose time. But I thought I would have been more excited than Fergus was if I were the one re-ceiving letters from her, and if I were the one sending letters to her, I would have hoped for more of a spark than I saw in her.

My understanding began to improve one afternoon when I found his front door open but the tobacco shop empty. I thought I heard voices in his living quarters, so I tiptoed back to the door and stood there.

It was the two of them. I could recognize their voices, but they were speaking in a low tone and I couldn't make out the words. I was disappointed that their conversation didn't seem to have any romance; if anything, it sounded like conspiracy.

All at once the voices took on a closing note, and before I could get away, the white doorknob turned and Fergus pulled the door open. He seemed surprised to see me but recovered right away.

"Hold it right there," he said. He looked over his shoulder and said in a lower voice, "It's just Alex. Go ahead."

My mouth was dry as he stepped forward and closed the door behind him. At the same time, I heard footsteps move away and the back door close.

"Come over here," he said. "You need to listen to me." He led the way to the card table, where he pulled out two chairs and we sat down. He held me with his eyes. "Now get this straight. Everything has seemed nice and jolly up until now, but things aren't what they seem. Not here, and not across the street. I'm workin' on a case that could be a matter of life and death. If it gets bungled, two things could happen. One, someone who ought to be hanged by the neck could get away free. Two, there's a person who might have no more of a chance than you would if an Apache was to drag you out of a root cellar."

"I'm sorry. I really am. I apologize. I would never do anything to give away you or—Miss Morrie."

He pointed his finger at me. "Don't say her name out loud to me, and don't say mine to her. We'll just say 'someone,' and we'll know what we mean. Have you got all of that?"

"Yes, sir."

"Good. Then you can still work for me."

* * * * *

Later that day he took me up to the crow's nest. "You've got a pretty good idea of who I'm keeping an eye on, haven't you?"

"Yes, I do."

"No names, of course. But when you're up here, you sit back from the window and watch what he does, what his wife does, and what the girl does."

"The girl."

"The blond one."

"Oh, the helper."

"That's right. Now, if anyone does anything remarkable, you remember the time. Or write it down. But don't write anything that has a clear reference, like a name or a description or an event. Nothing that can be traced. It's all on the up-and-up, I write my reports and send them away, but we don't leave something lying around that someone else could use."

"I understand."

"Now I'm going to go down and loaf in my shop like the happy-go-lucky feller that I am."

If it hadn't been for Evelyn, I don't know if I would have believed him a hundred percent. He was so good at playing the part of the easy-going borderline gambler, making pitter-patter conversation as the chips rattled, that I could have believed he had some of it in his blood. But Evelyn made up for any doubt. If she and Fergus were in on this case together, I was sure it was what he made it out to be. Dead serious and on the up-and-up.

As I watched the people across the street, I became convinced that something shady was going on with them. The barber didn't have much business, and he wasn't the type to have loafers hanging around to play checkers and to chin about the weather. He was restless. Every five or ten minutes he would come to the open doorway, poke his nose out, and look up and down the street. When someone went into his wife's shop, he would wander out onto the sidewalk and glance in.

The wife, meanwhile, hardly ever saw the light of day. I had noticed it before. The only time I had seen her was when she came out with a shopping bag and wasted no time going to the meat market and the general store. On the first day at my post, neither she nor the blond girl came outside at all.

On the second day, Evelyn stepped into view. She was carrying a lavender-colored scarf as she crossed the street and went into the seamstress' shop. Like clockwork, or rather like a chicken hawk coming out of a cuckoo clock, Mudrick came out of his barber shop, took a few steps to his left, then made a slow turn-around and went back. A few minutes later, Evelyn left the other woman's shop and crossed the street at a casual pace with the lavender scarf streaming. Mudrick closed his door and disappeared into the back of his shop, where I imagined he crossed over to talk to his wife.

* * * * *

I fed the kitchen scraps to Mrs. Colby's chickens and went out to the main street. I turned left, thinking I would check in on Evelyn. She had left the boarding house earlier, so I expected her to be in her shop. But when I got there, the door was closed. I pushed on the thumb latch, and it was locked.

I walked a couple of doors down until I came to the tobacco shop, and it was closed as well. I went on, wishing I hadn't tried both doors in plain view. Though I did have the self-control not to turn around and look, I was sure Mudrick had watched me.

At the end of the block I turned left, then turned again in the alley. As I came near the back door of Fergus' place, I took soft steps. Someone was inside.

I held still and listened, and a chill went over me. I heard sounds that I understood though I had never heard them before, sounds that I might have expected to hear the day I stood inside and listened. Here was the spark, the interest, that was missing when I delivered the first letters.

The chill passed, and I felt ashamed at standing in full daylight with my head turned to listen. It was none of my business, and fond as I was of her, I knew I was but a boy in her eyes as well as his. If I had thought about it ahead of time I might have expected to feel jealous or betrayed, but as it was, I knew I had no business there. I turned and went back the way I came.

* * * * *

As I was at my lookout post later the same day, I saw a caravan of wagons, some canvas-covered and some in the shape of large wooden boxes. On the sides of most of the wagons, faded red and yellow lettering proclaimed, "Hogan and Hogan," with the words "Shows and Spectacles" beneath. I had not seen one of these shows before, but I had heard of them, and I imagined that inside those wagons were tattooed ladies, snake charmers, and two-headed chickens.

When I told Fergus about the show, he said, "Oh, I know. Did you want to go to it?"

I didn't answer.

"Look," he said, "I'll close up for a few hours, and we'll go see it. Buy some snake-oil medicine, see the boxing midgets or the pickled head of some outlaw."

I felt as if I had a bad taste in my mouth. The wagons had looked shabby, and the men driving them had been swarthy and filmy. The idea of seeing grotesques did not appeal to me. "I don't know," I said.

"Let's go. We don't have to stay if we don't like it."

I felt that he wanted to be generous to me, maybe because of his sense of how he was getting along with Evelyn and how I might be aware of it. I said, "Oh, all right."

It turned out to be not so bad. All of the spectacles were in tents, and not very large ones, so I didn't have to look at anything I didn't want to. We decided to see a knife-thrower, and he was very good. His assistant, Miss Rachel, was tied to a circular wooden backboard that went round and round, while the man threw his knives and sunk them into the wood near her head, arms, and legs. After that we went to a kinetoscope, or peep-show as I heard it called. There I looked into a machine and turned the handle. The first one had a well-dressed man and woman dancing, and the second one had a cowboy riding a bucking bronco. The dancing didn't seem to begin or end, but the bronco-riding did. The rider climbed aboard, stayed on for several jumps, and got bucked off. Then with a flicker the story started over as he climbed on and went through it again.

By the time we had seen the shows and eaten some ice cream, night had fallen. The showmen had put out lanterns, and the air was full of bugs. As Fergus and I walked back into town, the main street was quiet.

When we came to the boarding house he said, "Probably won't have much business tonight. No need for you to waste your time."

I thanked him for taking me to the show, and I went inside. Mrs. Colby was the only one at home. She said Miss Morrie had gone to the show a little earlier, but I hadn't seen her. As before, I told myself it was none of my business.

* * * * *

The hot, dusty days dragged on. By my calculation, Fergus had been in town about a month, and I wondered how long he was going to spend at collecting observations. Then on one day that seemed no different from the others, things changed.

Mrs. Mudrick with her pale face and shifty glance left her seamstress shop in the middle of the afternoon. I could see the blond hair of the working girl, who watched the front part of the shop when the older woman went out.

Two or three minutes later, Evelyn crossed the street, this time carrying a black-and-silver shawl. As soon as she went into the shop, Mudrick the hawk came out of his. He stood in profile at the edge of the window, and his head went up. Then he turned and went back into his place. When Evelyn came out, he appeared in his doorway and stared at her as she crossed the street. My heartbeat picked up, and my mouth was dry. I could feel the malice from where I sat, and I feared for Evelyn. She was plucky, though, and she moved in her casual way without looking back.

Less than ten minutes later, Mrs. Mudrick returned with her shopping bag full of provisions. As she went in through the front door, the barber closed his door and withdrew into the back part of his shop.

I watched for the rest of the afternoon, and nothing out of the ordinary happened. The barber and the seamstress closed up their shops at six, and I saw no more of Evelyn. When I went downstairs to report to Fergus, he was gone.

I went to the boarding house, where Mrs. Colby had me bring in some coal. After that I took scraps to the chickens, washed up, and ate my supper in the kitchen. All this time I kept an eye out for Evelyn, but I did not see her.

When I went back to Fergus' establishment to help him with the evening's work, the front door was locked.

They were in conference, I thought, like the first time I overheard them and maybe like the second time. But I felt there was something in the air. They would make their move soon.

* * * * *

In the morning I found the door open, with Fergus in the crow's nest and a coffee cup in front of him. I went up the stairs.

"They should have opened up by now," he said.

I gave him my report from the day before.

He drummed his fingers on the table. "It's about what I would expect. But I don't like it that they haven't opened for business yet." He drummed again. "Look here, Alex. Why don't you go out and mosey around back of their place? See what you can, and come back here through the back door. I'll have it unlocked."

I did as he said. I went out the front door, turned left, walked to the end of the block, and crossed the main street. I wandered back to the alley and followed it behind the barber shop and the locale next door. I saw no sign of life—no clothes hanging out to dry, no door or window open, no kittens playing on the back steps. I recognized the place where, years earlier, I had seen a wagon deliver a dead man, but that was two barbers ago. The scene now was quiet and empty.

Fergus met me at the back door of his quarters and ushered me into the store. In a low voice, he said, "Tell me what you saw."

"Nothing," I said. "I didn't hear or see anything."

He smashed his palm with his fist. "I wonder if they've pulled out already. Damn it all." He narrowed his eyes on me. "Go ask at the livery stable. I don't think he had his own horses or a carriage, but find out what you can."

"Go out the front door?"

"Yeah, come and go that way. I don't think anyone's watching any more."

The man at the livery stable said the Mudricks had hired a carriage the evening before. They had a family emergency in Salt Lake, and they arranged to leave the carriage in Shelton where they would catch the train.

When I reported to Fergus, he tugged at the corner of his mustache. "Shelton. That's over a day's drive for them. If we move fast, we might catch 'em before they make it to the train." He gave me an appraising look. "Can you ride?"

"I know how."

"Well, get yourself a hat and a jacket, and ask Mrs. Colby to pack us some food. Don't say why. Just tell her we're going on a day's ride. I'd like to pull out of here in fifteen minutes."

"How about someone else? Do you have a message for her?"

"I'll tell her myself. I think the game's up, as far as secrecy goes."

* * * * *

Fergus was saddling his dark horse when I met him at the stable. He was dressed in his riding clothes as I had seen him the first day, and he was wearing a six-gun. A rifle and scabbard came into view when he turned away to fetch the bridle.

As he worked the bit into the horse's mouth, he said, "I should have been riding these horses more. I haven't ridden 'em but a couple of times in the last month, and they've gotten fat." He pulled the headstall over the horse's ears. "That sorrel's pretty gentle, though. You can get on him any day of the year." He untied the rope from the dark horse's neck and from the stall, coiled it, and tied it onto the right side of the saddle. "Here," he said, handing me the reins, "lead him outside."

Five minutes later he led the sorrel into the sunlight. I held up the cloth sack with the bread and meat Mrs. Colby had packed for us.

"What about this?"

"Give it here. I'll roll it up in your jacket and tie it on back." He pulled the reins from my hand as I started to take off my jacket. "Come on," he said. "We need to adjust your stirrups, too."

He wasted no motions as he made the bundle, tied it on, and measured the stirrup length against my outstretched arm. He held the sorrel and gave me a boost, then told me to stand in the stirrups.

"They fit all right," he said. He handed me the reins. "Don't fall off. We don't have time." He set his own reins, pulling the dark horse's head to the left, and swung aboard. In another minute we were on a fast walk out of Silverthorne.

"Is this your saddle?" I asked.

"No, I rented it."

"Don't you think I'll slow you down?"

"Not if you hang on. As soon as these horses warm up, we'll lope for a while."

"I don't know how much good I'll be. If we catch up with them, I mean."

"If things go wrong, you'll have to beat 'em to Shelton."

"If things go wrong?"

"This fella can be dangerous if he gets cornered. And I haven't done anything right for a while." He reached forward and felt the dark horse's neck. "Hell of a way to get these horses in shape." A minute later he said, "Let's lope."

231

The sorrel had an easy gait, and the motion seemed like a dream for several minutes until Fergus slowed us, jolting, to a walk. The horses were breathing hard, and the smell of their sweaty warmth rose in the air. After a mile of walking, we loped again.

That was the way we traveled, walking for a long while and loping for a short one. The sun climbed in the sky and heated up the day. The smell of sagebrush mixed with the dust and the odor of warm horses. The country had gone dry in late summer, with heat shimmering from the dull landscape, and antelope made small white dots in the distance.

When the sun was straight up, Fergus brought us to a halt. He pointed to the side of the trail.

"Looked like they stopped here. I'd guess about midnight."

I saw damp spots where the passengers had tinkled.

"Doesn't look like they stayed the night," he said. "But sooner or later they'll have to rest those horses. Of course, so will we."

An hour later, we came to a place where the trail went down through a grassy creek bottom. A few box elders grew in a wide spot, and a thin trickle ran through the middle. We dismounted there. Fergus loosened the cinches, and as the horses drank, we rested in the shade of the low trees.

"I haven't had anything to eat yet today," he said. "We might as well have some of that grub."

I was always ready to eat, so I untied the bundle.

With his fingertips and the heel of his hand, Fergus broke off an even piece of bread. As he handed the loaf to me, I asked what I had been wondering all along.

"What did the barber do that was so bad?"

He paused with the bread in his hand. "It's an ugly thing, Alex. But in my line of work, that's what I deal with." He reached for a slice of meat, laid it on the bread, and took a bite. When he had swallowed, he shook his head and spoke again. "To say the least, it's not normal. What this fella did is, he kidnapped that girl, with the help of his wife, and he's kept her for his own purposes."

"How long ago was that?"

"It's been over six years. You see, those two little girls are his."

A prickly sensation went up the back of my neck. I said, "Why would his wife do something like that? And why would the girl go along with it? You'd think she'd just run across the street at some point."

Fergus took another bite and waited to answer. "Like I said, it's far from normal. But it's not the first time people have done something like this, and I imagine it's not the last. People get into situations where they live in their own narrow way, and they have a sense of loyalty that's hard for someone like you or me to make sense of. But it runs deep. A fellow like this one has got a strange power."

My mouth was dry, and I felt like I couldn't get my full breath. "Why does he dye his hair?"

"So he won't look so much like the little girls."

I shook my head to keep from drifting. "But he's over fifty."

"He's fifty-four. And the girl is barely twenty."

I thought for a couple of seconds. "If you know this much, why hasn't anyone caught him?"

"The police bungled it. First in Pittsburgh and then in Cincinnati. I work for an agency, and we do things different."

"What took you so long once you tracked him to Silverthorne?"

"We had to be sure of the girl's identity."

"And that's what Evelyn, Miss Morrie, did yesterday?"

"That's right. I was going to send for the law this morning, and we were going to carry on like usual until they got there. I didn't think he'd bolt like he did. My mistake."

"So you don't have the authority to arrest him."

"No, but if I can get him collared in Shelton, or even before that, we can hold him whatever way we have to until we get a lawman. Shelton's a good place. It's got a sheriff as well as a telegraph and a train station." He motioned with his head. "You'd better eat somethin'. We've got a long ride ahead."

* * * * *

As we rode west through the afternoon, the hills grew closer together. Grassy slopes gave way to ridges, rocky and brushy with scattered cedars. Heat reflected from the rocks around us as well as from the dirt below. We came to a narrow passage where the air was even warmer. The carriage tracks led ahead.

Fergus and the dark horse rode forward, and I let the sorrel follow on the right with his nose even with the other horse's hip.

My eyes were squinting and my lips were parched. The air was heavy, and I swayed with the motion of the horse. Then everything happened at once—the ping of a ricochet, fragments of rock spraying out, the crash of a rifle shot, and the sorrel horse rearing up with its mane in my face. I lost my stirrups and my grip on the saddle horn, and I slid off the horse's hind end. His hooves kicked dirt in my face as he pounded away.

The dark horse was coming back. It was Fergus, leaning low in the saddle with his left hand reaching down to me.

"Grab a hold," he yelled.

We latched onto each other, he swung his arm and I swung my legs, and I pulled myself the rest of the way on. He turned the horse around again, and we galloped after the sorrel as two more shots rang out.

Half a mile ahead, the land opened up. Fergus slowed the horse to a walk, and we sidled up to the sorrel where he was cropping grass. I slid off and grabbed the loose reins, and Fergus dismounted.

"I was hoping it wouldn't come to this," he said. His eyes were narrowed, and he was glancing around. "Take down your rope. We're going to have to tie these horses."

We picketed the horses twenty yards apart, each to a clump of sagebrush. Fergus unbuckled his spurs and put them in his saddlebag. Then he pulled the rifle from the scabbard.

"Let's go."

I followed him to the northeast. I could see that his plan was to come around in back of Mudrick and try to get the drop on him.

It must have been five in the afternoon. Even out of the canyon, the air was breathless, and I sweated as I labored up the hillside. When we were almost to the crest, Fergus handed me the rifle and his hat, then got down on all fours and crawled to the very top. He came back shaking his head, and when I gave him the hat and rifle we moved on. He went through the maneuver two more times, and on his third sneak he sank low and settled back.

He made a hand signal for me to come up to him, so I did.

He spoke in a whisper. "He's right down below there. I'm going to go after him."

"What do you want me to do?"

He took his hat and put it on. "Just stand here and hang onto that rifle. Don't shoot unless he comes straight at you."

"But you're going to—"

"Listen to me. If I go down, you get the hell out of here and ride to Shelton. You tell the sheriff everything."

"Why don't we do that now?"

Fergus gave me a stare and said, "For the same reason I didn't earlier. This is my case, and I want to bring this son of a bitch to justice if I can. And besides, if I leave it all up to the law, they might let him get away clean again. I just hope he doesn't get away if he shoots me." Fergus was silent for a few seconds, as if he was thinking, and then he said, "The best way would be to bring him in alive, but I don't know how easy that'll be now." He turned away, then went up and over the top.

I stood there as he told me, holding the gun. Within half a minute I heard a shot, and I froze. I was sure Mudrick was the one who fired. The gunshot sounded like a rifle, and even if it was a pistol, I didn't think Fergus would have shot the man right away.

I needed to take a look. I inched forward until the canyon and then the hillside below me came into view. Fergus and Mudrick were in a tangle about forty yards down the slope. A rifle lay on the ground nearby, and the men's hats had rolled off to either side.

I expected Fergus to come out on top, get the man in a hammerlock, and have him under control. But this was no easy fight. Legs kicked, and arms flailed. Both men threw short, glancing punches. For his age and build, Mudrick had surprising strength. He not only held his own in the scuffle, but after a minute or so he got Fergus in what looked like an iron grip. He clawed at Fergus' cheek, pulling his eyelid down, while Fergus leaned his head back and away. With his left hand, Mudrick grabbed Fergus by the hair and then slipped his right arm across Fergus' throat. Mudrick shifted onto his butt and pushed back with his feet, tightening the stranglehold as Fergus tore at the man's arm. Mudrick reached across Fergus' body for the pistol, but Fergus pulled the hand away. Mudrick reached again and laid his fingers on the handle, but he couldn't pull the gun loose.

I raised the rifle and lined up the sights, but the barrel wavered and both men moved in and out of my line of fire. I lowered the gun.

Mudrick pulled the pistol from the holster, but it fell in the dirt. As he shifted to reach for it, Fergus broke free. He rolled over, then dove at Mudrick and stayed on top. Mudrick's fingers wriggled, but the six-gun was out of reach. Fergus settled his hands on the man's throat and said, "Are you ready to give up?"

Mudrick said something I didn't catch. Then he bucked with his body and raised his knee into Fergus's groin, throwing him halfway off. He reached again for the pistol that lay in the dirt.

Fergus came back on top, punched Mudrick hard in the face, and got both hands on his throat. Mudrick raised his left hand to poke a finger into Fergus's eye, while his right hand was out of sight. It looked as if he had a grip on Fergus's crotch. Fergus showed pain in his face, but he did not let up. He slammed Mudrick's head against the hard, rocky ground a dozen times until the man went limp.

With the rifle in my hands, I ran the short way down the hill. Fergus was rising to his feet when I got there. His right cheek had claw marks below the eye, and dirt clung to his face as well as to his hair and clothes. He leaned forward and was breathing hard.

"He's done for, isn't he?" I said.

Fergus nodded, then stood up straight. "I might have been able to do it the other way, bring him in alive, but I don't know. It would have been a hell of a lot harder. He didn't give me much choice." Fergus's chest heaved. "He had a lot of fight to him."

* * * * *

Back in Silverthorne, the news had arrived ahead of us. Mrs. Colby knew all about Mudrick's death, his wife being arrested, and the girl Polly and her two little ones being taken into custody.

"This is not good," she said as I ate my breakfast. "You say you're going out for a day's ride and you're gone for three, mixing up with criminals and almost getting your head shot off. I think you should stay away from that man Fergus."

"Well, he's leaving anyway. But I need to see him before he goes." I finished my breakfast alone and went out.

Fergus was sitting at his card table with a cup of coffee. "Thanks for coming," he said. "Sit down."

I took the chair next to him.

"I guess we need to tidy things up." He glanced around at his tobacco inventory. "Someone will come for this stuff, and for the books and what-not at her place." He laid a five-dollar gold piece on the table in front of me. "I'd appreciate it if you could look after things until they get here, and then help 'em pack up."

"I can do that. Are you both leaving pretty soon, then?"

"Oh, she's already gone."

My head came up. "Are you going to meet her some place?"

"Oh, no. Things can't work that way."

"Why?"

Fergus tipped his head. "If two people are married and in the same business, it's more dangerous for both of 'em and makes 'em less effective."

"But you seemed to get along so well together. You made such a good pair."

He shrugged. "As much as I don't like to admit it, we all make mistakes."

I thought about my spying, and I nodded.

Fergus went on. "It's hard to have perfect judgment and stick to it when the thing that isn't perfect still seems right."

It took me a few seconds to absorb that. When I did, I said, "So what will she do?"

"Pretty much the same as I will. Go where the next case is. But it probably won't be the same one as mine."

There was not much more after that. He packed his things and led the horses into the middle of the street. For the first and last time, he shook my hand.

"So long, Alex. Be good."

"I will," I said. "Thanks."

He got the horses into position, swung aboard the dark one, and lined out the packhorse. He rode out of Silverthorne the way he came in, but with the canvas packs quite a bit smaller. He turned once in the saddle and waved, and I waved back.

Blue Horse Mesa
Author's Note

The story of the Johnson County War of 1892 is well known in the history of Wyoming, as is the bravery of Nate Champion, who stood off an army of hired guns for the better part of a day until they smoked him out of a cabin and shot him down. The most eloquent part of the story is his own courage, which had fifty witnesses, but history has also preserved the contents of a little notebook that Champion kept while he was under siege.

Several years back, I heard a less verifiable story from the great writer Frederick Manfred, who in the mid-1950's interviewed people in Johnson County who were close in time and family to the original participants in the conflict. According to Manfred (whose research culminated in his novel *Riders of Judgment*), there was speculation that Nate Champion might have had a child with a woman who was married to someone else. With all respect to a brave man, the following story explores that possible lost trail.

Blue Horse Mesa

Nate Champion rode down from Blue Horse Mesa on a buckskin he called Tag. Of the half-dozen horses in his string, Nate liked the deep-chested buckskin the best for traveling across country. Tag with his smooth lope put the miles behind them. Now the horse was picking his way down the southern slope, where the pale sun of late March had melted snow on the rocks along the trail.

Lone country, it seemed today. In the ten or twelve miles since he left Powder River, he had seen few tracks in the snow. Up on top, he had seen nothing. As he leaned back in the saddle and shifted with the movements of the horse, he felt the pangs of hunger and along with them the downcast feeling that sometimes came at this time of day. He didn't worry about a small thing like that, though; he could ride all day without eating, and he would usually get a second wind in the afternoon.

There was plenty else to worry about. Talk had it that Frank Canton had a dead list of seventy men in the Powder River country. Some said only twenty, and others said there was no such a thing. Nate didn't even know where Canton was, but he figured if there was any list at all, no matter how short, the name of Nate Champion would be on it. That was one thing to worry about—it could come at any time, a bullet in the back like they did to John Tisdale. Nate was a long ways off his regular range for someone to be stalking him here, and he had kept a good eye on his backtrail all the way over, but once the big cattlemen got started, they knew no stopping.

The other thing to worry about was Lou Ellen. He hadn't seen her since October. Over a period of months they had met more than a dozen times on Blue Horse Mesa—never for very long, but the feeling ran so deep that he felt it would never end. Sometimes it took her an hour or so longer to get away, but she always made it to their rendezvous—until the last time, when she didn't show up at all. Since then, he hadn't heard a word from her. Between that and the trouble with Canton and the others, it had been a long winter.

Down off the slope and headed back west again, he caught the smell of woodsmoke. Cottonwood Creek lay up ahead. If he could get a look at the camp, he could decide whether to ride in or go around.

Clearing a rise just enough to look over, Nate saw a picket line with a half-dozen horses tied to it. Closer to the creek stood a low canvas tent with a pile of firewood on one side and a freight wagon covered with a tarpaulin on the other. A grey-bearded man in a wool cap came out of the tent, straightened up, and looked around. When Nate got a full view of the man's face, he recognized him as Ben Jones, the chuckwagon cook. He and another roundup hand, Bill Walker, trapped through the winter, so this would be their current camp.

Nate gave the buckskin a nudge, then rode into plain view and gave Ben a wave. At the edge of the camp he swung down and covered the last ten yards on foot.

"Howdy, Nate," called the older man.

"Hello, Ben. Havin' any luck?"

"Oh, a little. And yourself?"

"Same." Nate glanced around the camp. "Where's Bill?"

"He's downstream. We'll see about makin' one more set here before we move on." Ben tugged on the bill of his wool cap. "Care for a cup of coffee? Somethin' to eat?"

Nate shrugged. "I wouldn't turn down either."

"Tie up your horse, then, and I'll get you somethin'."

Seated on a log with a tin plate balanced on his lap, Nate broke apart a biscuit and poured a dab of molasses on each half. "Well, what's new?"

"Not much with me. Heard about you, though."

"Oh, really? What was that?"

"Heard they come callin' for you one morning, while you were still in bed."

"That they did."

"Heard it was Canton and Elliott and two others."

"I knew Elliott for certain, and I'm pretty sure of the rest."

"Hah!" Ben poured coffee into a tin cup and then took a seat on the same log. "How about that fella that was bunkin' with you?"

"Gilbertson? He's not much of a fighter. I threw what lead I could."

"You didn't get anyone, though?"

"I drew some blood on someone, but that's all I know."

"These big cattlemen just don't want you independents to have your own roundup, do they?"

"If that was all it was. But there's other bad blood, and it just got worse when they couldn't get me."

"You mean Tisdale."

"He had an old grudge against Canton, from back in the Texas days. First thing I did, when I could see they weren't comin' after me again, was ride across country to his place. Soon as I got there, I told him, 'There's goin' to be trouble.' He was worried, I could tell, and there was his wife, she hadn't had the baby yet, but he said, 'By God, if we've got to fight, that's what we do.'"

"And he didn't live to see Christmas."

"No, and sometimes I think it's my fault."

"For goin' to tell him?"

"More than that. Not long after these fellas tried to jump me, John Tisdale and I run into Make Shonsey."

"That two-faced son of a bitch."

"The same. Well, I knew that Shonsey knew who took the shots at me, because I tracked 'em back to a camp right next to the NH, where he's foreman. And he'd been by, all smiles, just the day before. So I knew he knew, and I made him say all four names in front of John Tisdale, in case something happened to me."

"So Shonsey talked?"

"He had to." Nate patted the grip of his six-gun. "But he hated to say it in front of John, who despised Canton already."

"Well, hell, then, it just gave Frank one more reason to shoot him in the back."

"Seems like it now, and no one doubts that Canton shot him. But you've got a man who salted his alibi every way he could, and eyewitnesses afraid to stick to their story."

"Should be an open-and-shut case."

Nate took a drink of coffee. "Not when you've got all the big mucky-mucks on your side. He walks free on the first warrant, and the governor won't have him brought back from Illinois on the second one."

The older man took out a pipe and began scraping the bowl with his jack knife. "Maybe they think they've gone far enough."

"No tellin'." Nate started on the second half of his biscuit. "How long you been trappin' over this way?"

"'Bout a month."

"Catchin' mostly what?"

"Coyotes." Ben turned the pipe upside down and rapped it on the log.

Nate decided to take a chance. "Seen anything of Spangler?"

"He sold out to Irvine."

Nate stopped with the biscuit halfway to his mouth. "He did?"

"Yep. Sold what he could, and moved to Douglas." The older man made a crackling sound as he blew air through the stem of his pipe. "His wife had a little one, you know. He moved 'em into a town."

"Not afraid of the trouble, I wouldn't think. He's careful to stay on good terms with everyone. When did he move?"

"'Long about a month ago."

"Huh."

Ben stuffed fresh tobacco into the bowl of his pipe. "You fellas still gonna go ahead with your independent roundup, eh?"

Nate ran his tongue around to clean his teeth. "I suppose so. You can't say you're goin' to do somethin', and then not do it."

"That's right. And you got Jack Flagg and all the Hat boys behind you."

"Sure. That's all fine and good, if your friends are around. But even when they are, if it comes to the scratch, it's what a man can do for himself. He's got to. He just hopes he gets a chance, more than some did."

The older man lit his pipe and smoked in silence while Nate finished the second biscuit.

"Want more coffee?"

"No, thanks. I should probably move on."

Ben looked at the sky. "Don't let me keep you. Be dark sooner'n you know."

"Hate to be in a hurry."

"Not at all. Make use of the daylight."

Nate stood up. "Well, I thank you for the grub."

"Wasn't much."

"It was good all the same." Nate shook the grounds out of his cup. "If you and Bill get over to the KC, don't be shy. I'm stayin' in the cabin there, and you fellas are always welcome."

"That's not where they jumped you?"

"Nah, that was out on the Bar C. This one's not so out of the way, and it's a little more comfortable. Don't be afraid to stop in."

"We won't." The old man stood up and took a cheerful puff on his pipe.

"So long, then." Nate checked the cinch on his horse and swung aboard. He touched his hat in farewell, then put the buckskin into a trot.

So Lou Ellen got moved to Douglas. There wasn't much chance of seeing her again on Blue Horse Mesa, and there was no telling if he would see her elsewhere anytime soon. It always seemed like the real thing when he was with her, but after all she was married, and even if Nate didn't care much for Spangler, he didn't like the feeling of doing another man wrong. If he had gone this long without seeing her, maybe it was just as well if it stayed that way.

On the other hand, he didn't like to leave things unresolved. She'd had a baby. He needed at least to be able to ask her about that.

Maybe later. This business with Canton and the others had him looking over his shoulder all the time. When he told John Tisdale there was going to be trouble, he didn't know how much. He still didn't.

* * * * *

Lou Ellen stood at the window and watched the afternoon outside turn grey. One day seemed no different from the next, and she had felt numb, dead of feeling, ever since Chas had moved them to this town. She didn't think it was the baby. Some women talked about a depressed feeling that set in after giving birth, but this felt like something else. It was as if something had died inside her, something that had kept her going.

For the last year she had harbored the guilty feeling that came from knowing she could never love her husband as much as she had loved Nate Champion. But the guilt never outweighed the desire, never kept her from wanting to see him again.

Sometimes he rode a sorrel, sometimes a white horse, most of the time a buckskin, but she always knew him from a distance. She knew his posture, his stocky build set off with a dark hat and a dark shirt. As he came closer, her heart raced. Even with his face shaded by his hatbrim, she could make out his full mustache, dark eyebrows, and searching eyes. He reined his horse in and swung down, light as a cat, the white handle on his revolver swaying, the steely blue-grey eyes meeting hers. Then he held her in his arms with all the strength of a man of the earth. When she took him to her, the mingled smells of the felt hat, the wool shirt, and the leather chaps worked like an aphrodisiac.

How many times? She had not counted, and he said he hadn't either. It was all open and free, each time unto itself, with no thought of anything ever being different.

Then she would have to leave. It was always her obligations that brought their meetings to an end. She stretched it, for one minute more, and then she had to hurry away, leaving him there on the mesa standing by his horse and holding the reins.

Back at the ranch house, she would bide her time and count the days until the next visit. Sometimes the thought stole upon her that she might have seen him for the last time, and it chilled her heart. But when the appointed day came around, there he was again, sometimes waiting, sometimes riding across Blue Horse Mesa.

It was always that way, the cycle of guilt and hope and fear and escape, one more time in his arms, until one day Chas told her he knew.

She had broken the news about her carrying a child, and he told her he thought it might not be his.

"You're not going to see him again," was the decree.

"You speak as if you owned me."

"I don't have to. But I'm telling you what you're not going to do."

"And if I decide for myself?"

"Things will happen otherwise. Believe me."

Now she was living in this dusty town, where even the snow was dirty. Chas delivered coal and drank two quarts of beer at home every night. The baby cried. Lou Ellen rinsed the diapers, hung them on the rack to dry, and stared out the window.

She hadn't gotten to see him that last time, not even to explain. She had left him waiting. Worse than anything, she did not have the certain feeling that she would see him again to make things right.

Chas, meanwhile, acted as if nothing had happened. He spoke of Frank Canton, Major Wolcott, and Senator Carey as if they were all old friends. The only one she knew was Canton, who had stopped by the ranch in November. An oily man in a curved-brim hat and a long topcoat, he had a sliding pair of eyes that took in everything. Some friend. If she hadn't begun to show already, he would have laid a hand on her when

Chas went to the outhouse. That was the feeling he gave her. Now Chas said that Canton and Wolcott and some others were coming through on the train, and he hoped he got a chance to see them.

A few thin snowflakes drifted past the window. She wondered where Nate was at this moment. Probably out on the range somewhere. A thousand times she had imagined him waiting for her the day she stood him up—pacing, fretting, stretching it out for a few more minutes, then swinging onto his buckskin horse and riding back to the Middle Fork. She doubted he had come to Blue Horse Mesa many more times, but she had the conviction that he had done so at least once before she left the ranch.

* * * * *

Nate looked out the cabin door and watched the snow come down slantwise. After ten years in this country, he knew storms in early April could be as bad as any. Time to stay by the fire, even if it got a little close with the present company. Nick didn't have much of an odor himself, but the trappers were like others he had known. They got so they couldn't smell themselves. All the same, it was good to be able to offer them a place to roll out their blankets, and it gave him some comfort to have visitors. Not that company was any guarantee against getting attacked—he had learned that with Gilbertson—but it kept the mind from feeding on other things.

The old man, Ben, had a fiddle. He would probably play it tonight, and they could sing songs about devil horses and blue-eyed girls.

Snow was piling up on the tarpaulin that covered the trappers' wagon. No chores needed to be done. The men had a good stack of firewood inside, and the horses had hay. Still, Nate had a restless feeling, as if he should be doing something.

He closed the door and turned to join the company. The old man sat at the table slicing spuds, and his younger pal, the cowhand Bill Walker, had his stockinged feet propped up on a crate to catch the warmth of the stove. Nick Ray was sewing up a hole on a cotton sack he used for a gear bag.

"Still comin' down?" he asked.

"Kind of bitter," Nate answered. "Good night to be inside."

"Good weather for sleepin'," said the old man. "Bill here would like to be runnin' off to town, but I tell him there's time enough for that."

Bill swayed his head from side to side. "Tells me to keep a wrinkle in it, but that's easier for him than it is for me."

"Time you sell your furs," said Nick, "you'll still have a while to rustle some petticoats before roundup begins."

"That's my kind of rustlin'." Bill stopped, then added in a quick breath, "If you'll excuse my language."

"Hell, no," said Nick. "Bein' called a rustler in these parts is the next thing to a compliment. What it means is, you don't kiss the Association's ass. Call me a rustler, it means no one's gonna mistake me for a friend of Fred Hesse or W.C. Irvine, much less Mike Shonsey or Frank Canton."

Both the trappers gave a little laugh. Nate couldn't blame them for wanting to stay out of trouble. Come spring, they would want to hire on with an outfit, and chances were that they would work for some member of the Association. But on the hired man's level, no matter which brand he rode for, a fellow knew that the Association didn't run things fair and square.

Anyone who wasn't a member and owned cattle was presumed to be a rustler; he was blackballed from working for the big outfits. Members could brand mavericks and divvy them up, but a small operator wasn't supposed to brand even his own strays if they got off his land. That was the thing that galled most—the Wyoming Stock Growers Association claimed the right to rule the open range. Everyone knew it was crooked, but it was nothing for a chuckwagon cook or a circle rider to try to buck against.

* * * * *

Nate awoke in the cold grey of morning. The other men were still asleep. He could hear their breathing and snuffle-snoring. Someone needed to build up the fire in the stove, and he figured he might as well.

He dressed in a minute, put on his hat to keep his head warm, and went about starting a fire. As soon as Nate opened the door on the stove, the old man sat up in bed, his thin hair wisping out. As the one who always had to get up at three in the morning during roundup, he probably thought he should have gotten up first this morning.

"Go ahead and take it easy," said Nate. "No hurry on anything until I get a fire."

The old man settled back into his bed.

With splinters and kindling Nate got a blaze going, then fed on some thicker pieces. He broke the skim of ice on the water bucket and poured the last of the water into the coffee-pot. The fire was crackling now as it took off. Nate left the door of the stove open and pulled a chair up next to it.

The air in the room warmed up, and the other men came alive. The old man sat on the side of the bed and pulled his clothes on. Nick Ray yawned, then pulled the covers to his chin and lay with his eyes open. Bill called out for an order of ham and eggs.

"You'll get flapjacks if you're lucky," said Ben as he stood up and hunched into his coat. He put on his hat and crossed the room to warm his hands at the stove. "I suppose I should go get us a bucket of water."

"Sure." Nate poked another length of firewood into the heart of the fire.

The other two men got up and started milling around. Bill rolled a cigarette and smoked it, then tossed the butt into the stove.

"I wonder what's takin' Ben so long," he said.

Nate shrugged. "Might be makin' a deposit."

"Well, I'm gonna go take a look-see." Bill, who was already wearing his coat, put on his hat and gloves and went out.

"Let's go ahead and start fixin' breakfast," Nate said. "If Ben wants to make hotcakes when he gets back, that's fine, but we can fry up some spuds in the meanwhile."

He went to the dugout at the end of the cabin, selected a half-dozen potatoes, and carried them to the table. Nick was cutting slices off a slab of bacon.

By the time the skillet had heated up and the bacon had started to sizzle, neither of the trappers had come back.

"I wonder what's keepin' them two fellas," said Nick.

Nate frowned. "There might be someone out there holdin' 'em."

Nick stood up and said, "I think I'll go take a look." He picked up his rifle and headed for the door.

Nate had an uneasy feeling, but as he was busy poking at the bacon, he said, "All right, but look out."

A minute later, he heard the crash of a rifle shot and a hoarse cry. He jumped for his gunbelt where it hung looped on the bedpost, and he heard six or eight shots together. With his gun in hand, he ran to the door and peeked out.

Nick was ten yards out from the cabin, on his hands and knees, crawling toward the door.

A shot splintered the door jamb, and Nate ducked inside. He figured the men were shooting from the stable, so he fired in that direction and sank back. He opened the door to see how Nick was doing, and two slugs knocked chips of wood in his face. He slammed the door, opened it again, and blazed three more shots at the stable.

Nick, still crawling, had made it almost to the doorstep when a shot sounded and his back jerked, and he fell forward. Nate stuck his gun in his belt and leaned forward, and with bullets thudding into the lumber around him, he dragged Nick inside. The man was breathing and groaning, but he could not speak.

"I'm sorry, Nick. We should've known when the other two didn't come back."

A hail of bullets shattered the window and raised splinters on the back wall. Nate stayed low. He smelled smoke, and looking around, he saw where a bullet had punctured the stovepipe. Black smoke was curling up from the skillet as well. Ducking, he scurried to the stove, grabbed a rag from his chair, and pulled the skillet off the heat. He did the same with the coffeepot. He hadn't even had time to put in the grounds.

Another volley came in through the window, and he crouched to reload his pistol. Nick was still breathing in gasps.

It looked like one man against a bunch, and the idea began to settle in that he might not live to tell about it. He felt in his shirt pocket for his notebook and a stub of pencil, and under the date of April 9th he wrote as much as he could in the time he thought he could spare. He told how the attack started, and then he ended his entry:

Nick is shot but not dead yet. He is awful sick. I must go and wait on him.

Bullets came in at the window again. Nate went to the doorway and emptied his six-shooter, drawing fire. He ducked back and reloaded, then crawled to the other side of the cabin where his rifle stood against the wall. He stuck the pistol in his belt again and levered a shell into the Winchester.

For quite a while he traded shots, and when there came a lull, he wrote a few more words.

It is now about two hours since the first shot. Nick is still alive.

Then he had to put the notebook down for a minute to steady himself as another barrage of shots came.

They are still shooting and are all around the house. Boys, there is bullets coming in like hail.

Them fellows is in such shape I can't get at them. They are shooting from the stable and river and back of the house.

A stillness in the room caused him to crawl over to where Nick lay, and then he wrote a few more words.

Nick is dead. He died about 9 o'clock. I see a smoke down at the stable. I think they have fired it. I don't think they intend to let me get away this time.

Nate took a deep breath and looked over what he had written. Maybe Jack Flagg and the Hat boys would get to read this. Maybe not. Even if someone took it off his dead body, though, and burned it, these words would have been written. He could do that much.

He went back to trading shots, now at the window and now at the door, taking snap shots with the rifle and thinking he might have made a hit or two.

Things cooled down then, and a funny noise came at the door. He looked out the window to see someone had taken to throwing a rope. He didn't go for it. While he still had breath, he would put down a few more words.

> It is now about noon. There is someone at the stable yet. They are throwing a rope at the door and dragging it back. I guess it is to draw me out. I wish that duck would go further so I can get a shot at him.

> Boys, I don't know what they have done with them two fellows that stayed here last night.

> Boys, I feel pretty lonesome just now. I wish there was someone here with me so we could watch all sides at once. They may fool around till I get a good shot before they leave.

The ranch yard had gone quiet now—too quiet. As he craned his neck to look out the window from each side, he could see no movement. No telling how many men were out there. At least twenty, and not a flicker.

He sat on the floor by the table and took the skillet into his lap. The bacon, crisp on one side and fatty on the other, was cold on the tongue. The fire in the stove had long since gone out, and he couldn't imagine cooking anything anyway. He ate a couple of slices of raw potato, discolored now, and ran out of appetite. He poured warm water from the coffeepot and drank a cupful.

Time dragged on, and then he heard a commotion of yelling and shooting, but no bullets came his way. He went to the window and peeped out to see that a buckboard and rider had come by, and some of the gunmen had opened up on them. It looked as if at least one of the men had gotten away, but Nate couldn't be sure in all of the chaos.

A man came into view by the stable, barely within range. Nate took a shot, and the man disappeared. Silence settled in again, and Nate took the opportunity to scribble a few more words about the buckboard and the man at the stable. Then he choked at the next words but made himself write them.

It don't look as if there is much show of my getting away.

Before long, the men outside put the abandoned wagon to use. As it came into view, he saw they had heaped it with hay and chopped-up fence posts, and using the pile of hay for a cover, they were backing it toward the cabin. A rattle of bullets through the window kept him from getting any shots at them.

It didn't look good. They had him pinned down, and now they were pushing a go-devil at him. His heart was pounding and his mouth was dry as he took up the pencil and notebook. As he wrote, a volley of shots would come, then a pause, and then another barrage.

Well, they have just got through shelling the house again like hail. I heard them splitting wood. I guess they are going to fire the house tonight. I think I will make a break when night comes, if alive.

The gunfire kept him from looking out, but the smell of smoke coming in through the window made his heart sink. He wrote fast.

Shooting again. I think they will fire the house this time.

He was right. He could see the flames from the wagon as they licked up onto the eaves, caught the roof on fire, and then worked down the wall. In a matter of minutes, smoke was filling the room, getting thicker and lower. He had time to write one last bit, and then he was going to have to try to run for it.

It's not night yet. The house is all fired. Goodbye boys, if I never see you again.
                                        Nathan D. Champion

He tucked the notebook inside his shirt and tried to gather his wits. It was a good fifty yards to the ravine south of the house, and his best chance was without his boots. He pulled them off, straightened out his wool socks, pulled on another pair, and crawled to the back door. This was it. He either got away or he didn't, but they weren't going to burn him like a rat. He was all on his own. He hated to leave Nick's body in the fire, but it was the only way.

For one more time that day, he thought of people he might never see again—his brother Dudley, Lou Ellen. They would know he went down fighting. So would Jack Flagg and the boys. But none of them was here now.

He needed to get out of this smoke, or he wouldn't be able to breathe enough to run. With the six-gun tucked in his belt and the rifle in his hand, he pulled the door open and made a run for it.

The black smoke poured out around him, and he felt enormous energy as he took the first few strides. He heard shouts of "There he goes! There he goes!" and his mouth went dry as a tingling went through his shoulders and neck. He was running fine, though, his legs lifting and his lungs clearing.

As he pushed around the bend, a man appeared with a rifle, then another standing nearby, also aiming. Nate didn't have enough time to stop and draw a bead, and everything was out of order as he raised the rifle. A bullet tore into his arm and he dropped the gun. As he grabbed for his pistol, he felt three more slams in the chest, and he floated like nothing.

* * * * *

Lou Ellen held the baby in her arms as she looked in the store window at a pair of gloves—men's work gloves, with flared leather cuffs, the kind she had seen more than once on Blue Horse Mesa.

There was nothing left now, nothing but servitude, bitterness, and hatred. She could make peace with her husband and put in her time. She could bite her tongue when she heard him

261

and others talk about the rustler war. She could hate the cattlemen and their hired guns for not having to answer for what they did, for having the governor and the senators on their side, for doing as a group what none of them would dare on his own. When four couldn't do it, they hired fifty.

She could nurture all the contempt she wanted, but she knew it could not change what had happened. Nate Champion was worth any number of these shameless cowards, yet they went on living, many of them in prosperity. That was all she had, knowing that he was a better man— that, and a little baby named Chance, and the determination that some day when her life was her own, she would go one more time to Blue Horse Mesa.

About the Author

John D. Nesbitt lives in the plains country of Wyoming, where he teaches English and Spanish at Eastern Wyoming College. His articles, reviews, fiction, and poetry have appeared in numerous magazines and anthologies. He has had more than thirty books published, including short story collections, contemporary novels, and traditional westerns, as well as textbooks for his courses. John has won many awards for his work, including two awards from the Wyoming State Historical Society (for fiction), two awards from Wyoming Writers for encouragement of other writers and service to the organization, two Wyoming Arts Council literary fellowships (one for fiction, one for non-fiction), a Will Rogers Medallion Award for *Dark Prairie* (a frontier mystery) and another for *Thorns on the Rose* (a poetry collection), a Western Writers of America Spur finalist award for his novel *Raven Springs*, and the Spur award itself for his short story "At the End of the Orchard" and for his novels *Trouble at the Redstone* and *Stranger in Thunder Basin*. His recent work includes *Poacher's Moon,* a contemporary novel; *Blue Horse Mesa*, a collection of western stories; and *Field Work*, a retro-noir fiction collection. Visit his website at www.johndnesbitt.com

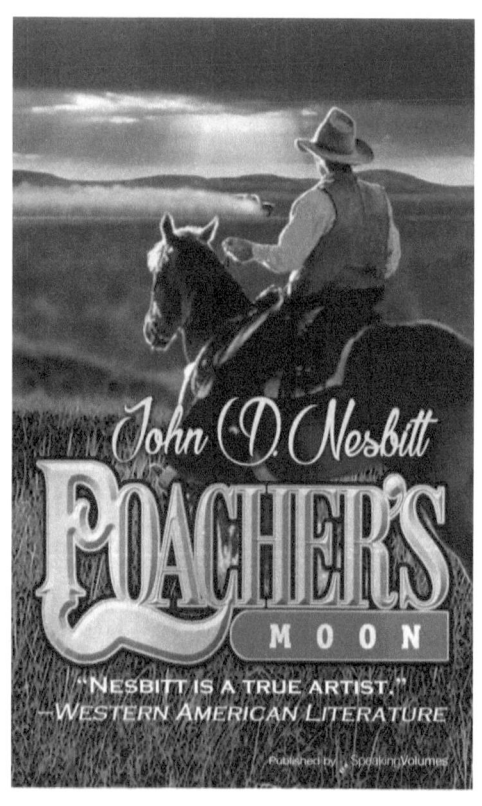

Visit us at

John D. Nesbitt

BLACK HAT
BUTTE

"NESBITT IS A TRUE ARTIST."
—WESTERN AMERICAN LITERATURE

Published by SpeakingVolumes

Visit us at www.speakingvolumes.us

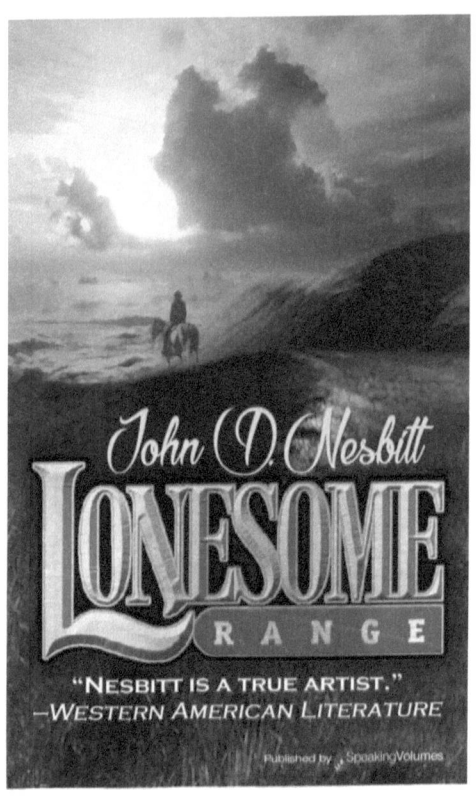

"NESBITT IS A TRUE ARTIST."
—WESTERN AMERICAN LITERATURE

Published by SpeakingVolumes

Visit us at www.speakingvolumes.us

"For the Norden Boys rings as true as a triangle around the chuckwagon at suppertime."
—*True West*

FOR THE NORDEN BOYS

JOHN D. NESBITT

Published by SpeakingVolumes

Visit us at www.speakingvolumes.us

Sign up for free and bargain books

Join the Speaking Volumes mailing list

Text

ILOVEBOOKS

to 22828 to get started.